PRAISE FOR

LUMBERJANES

THE MOON IS UP!

"This second volume in the middle-grade series maintains all of the best elements of both its prose predecessor and its comics roots, from its zippy signature argot (bons mots such as "Where the Roxane Gay are you going?") to a diverse cast of characters . . . More feisty feminist fun." —*Kirkus Reviews*

THE LUMBERJANES
NOVELS

LUMBERJANES

THE MOON IS UP

BOOK TWO

BY MARIKO TAMAKI
ILLUSTRATED BY BROOKLYN ALLEN

BASED ON THE LUMBERJANES COMICS
CREATED BY SHANNON WATTERS,
GRACE ELLIS, NOELLE STEVENSON & BROOKLYN ALLEN

AMULET BOOKS
NEW YORK

THE LIBRARY OF CONGRESS HAS CATALOGED THE HARDCOVER EDITION AS FOLLOWS: NAMES: TAMAKI, MARIKO, AUTHOR. | ALLEN, BROOKE A., ILLUSTRATOR. TITLE: LUMBERJANES: THE MOON IS UP / BY MARIKO TAMAKI ; ILLUSTRATED BY BROOKLYN ALLEN. OTHER TITLES: MOON IS UP | DESCRIPTION: NEW YORK : AMULET BOOKS, 2018. | SERIES: LUMBERJANES: BOOK 2 | "BASED ON THE LUMBERJANES COMICS CREATED BY SHANNON WATTERS, GRACE ELLIS, NOELLE STEVENSON & BROOKLYN ALLEN." IDENTIFIERS: LCCN 2017052449 | ISBN 9781419728686 (HARDCOVER POB) CLASSIFICATION: LCC PZ7.T1587 LUK 2018 | DDC [FIC]--DC23

PAPERBACK ISBN 978-1-4197-3951-4

TEXT COPYRIGHT © 2018 BOOM! STUDIOS
BOOK DESIGN BY SIOBHAN GALLAGHER

PUBLISHED IN PAPERBACK IN 2019 BY AMULET BOOKS, AN IMPRINT OF ABRAMS. ORIGINALLY PUBLISHED IN HARDCOVER BY AMULET BOOKS IN 2018. ALL RIGHTS RESERVED. NO PORTION OF THIS BOOK MAY BE REPRODUCED, STORED IN A RETRIEVAL SYSTEM, OR TRANSMITTED IN ANY FORM OR BY ANY MEANS, MECHANICAL, ELECTRONIC, PHOTOCOPYING, RECORDING, OR OTHERWISE, WITHOUT WRITTEN PERMISSION FROM THE PUBLISHER.

PRINTED AND BOUND IN U.S.A.
10 9 8 7 6 5 4 3 2 1

AMULET BOOKS ARE AVAILABLE AT SPECIAL DISCOUNTS WHEN PURCHASED IN QUANTITY FOR PREMIUMS AND PROMOTIONS AS WELL AS FUNDRAISING OR EDUCATIONAL USE. SPECIAL EDITIONS CAN ALSO BE CREATED TO SPECIFICATION. FOR DETAILS, CONTACT SPECIALSALES@ABRAMSBOOKS.COM OR THE ADDRESS BELOW.

AMULET BOOKS® IS A REGISTERED TRADEMARK OF HARRY N. ABRAMS, INC.

ABRAMS The Art of Books
195 Broadway, New York, NY 10007
abramsbooks.com

FOR JAKE AND ALEX.
—M.T.
TO MY LOVE, SHAWNEE,
AND OUR FOUR GLORIOUS
CHILDREN: LINUS,
SADIE-SUE, BAXTER,
AND PG.
—B.A.

LUMBERJANES

FIELD MANUAL

LUMBERJANES PLEDGE

I solemnly swear to do my best

Every day, and in all that I do,

To be brave and strong,

To be truthful and compassionate,

To be interesting and interested,

To pay attention and question

The world around me,

To think of others first,

To always help and protect my friends

~~To~~

THEN THERE'S A LINE ABOUT GOD, OR WHATEVER

And to make the world a better place

For Lumberjane scouts

And for everyone else.

PART ONE

ASTRONO-ME-ME-ME!

"OH MY STARS!"

The universe is a really, really, really big place, containing more than 100 billion galaxies, each containing more than 100 billion stars, including that great big star we call the Sun. In this way, the study of the universe provides scouts with a much-needed perspective on just how teeny tiny we really are in the grand context of things.

The study of celestial bodies has multiple benefits. Early Lumberjanes studied the stars to orient themselves and plot courses on land and sea. Knowing the location of the North Star can be helpful for finding your way home, or to your next adventure.

Ultimately, from planets to pulsars, the study of astronomy offers a glimpse into the real answer to the question, "Where are we?" Lumberjanes who have acquired this badge know the answer is . . .

CHAPTER 1

It was early morning at Miss Qiunzella Thiskwin Penniquiqul* Thistle Crumpet's camp for Hardcore Lady-Types, and Jo was lying on her bunk, arms tucked under her head, her brown eyes fixed on the ceiling . . . thinking.

Outside of camp, Jo could spend a whole day lost in thought. Which was a saying Jo didn't like, because it suggested that she was "lost" in thought. And she wasn't lost. She was just . . . thinking.

About what?

Many things, actually.

Including:

The mechanics of pulleys.

Whether she turned her alarm clock off before she left for camp.

* Pronounced *Penny-quee-quellle*

Whether she did or did not see a creature disembark from a moon-like structure a few days ago.

Also, Newton's Law of Motion.

To paraphrase, Newton's Law says that something will keep doing what it's doing, the way it's doing it, until another force shows up and says something like,

Today, this force was April, whose fierce green eyes, framed by her bright, cherry-red hair, peeked over Jo's bunk.

Her booming voice filled the cabin. "Are you ready to begin this, the next chapter in our most adventurous summer?!"

April, one of Jo's best friends since forever and a fellow member of Roanoke cabin, was often described as a force—a force to be reckoned with, a force of nature, and so on.

Today April was in a bit of a hurry because there was a lot to do and . . . Actually, there was always a lot to do. Actually, maybe April was always in a bit of a hurry.

Fortunately, being in a hurry and being a Lumberjane go very well together.

Jo sat up, her head skimming the roof of the cabin as she swung her legs over the side of her bunk. "Yes, I am."

"Indubitably!" April tightened the white bow tied around her hair. "Then let's make like a Lumberjane and get GOING!"

It was another amazingly gorgeous day, and outside the cabin the sky looked like a kid's drawing: deep blue, with three puffy clouds and a bright yellow sun shining down on the summer home away from home of the Lumberjanes.

Was this yet another great day to be a Lumberjane? Yes it was, because, and it's been said before but it is worth repeating, pretty much every day is a great day to be a Lumberjane.

April and Jo charged across the courtyard, past the fire pit and the flagpole, the volleyball nets and the picnic benches, toward the mess hall.

Technically, April was charging, Jo was strolling. Because

April had much shorter legs. Also April liked to CHARGE forward. Jo had very long legs, and she liked to stroll in long, loping strides, hands in pockets. It is a testament to Jo and April's long friendship that they knew how to walk at the exact same speed while walking with completely different paces and strides.

It was probably also a cornerstone of their friendship that April liked to talk as much as Jo liked to be quiet and think.

If Jo and April both liked to talk, it would be a very loud friendship.

April breathed in deeply. "This day is splendidly, vociferously, unquestionably fabulous, is it not? I believe it is."

Jo took a deep breath. It was true. The air smelled like pine, sunshine, and possibility.

Recently, the very adventurous members of Roanoke cabin—April, Jo, Mal, Molly, and Ripley—had charged up a mountain that didn't end up being a mountain but rather a frequently disappearing access route to a society of very laid-back cloud people called Cloudies. This adventure also involved discovering a herd of smelly but magical unicorns.

That was a pretty epic day.

And today was a new day.

And April was ready for more epic-ness.

April rubbed her hands together, her ruby hair glinting

in the sun. "Did you spend your morning of quiet reflection considering how we're going to totally kick butt at Galaxy Wars?"

April said it like a TV game show announcer. *GALAXY WAAARS!*

Jo smiled. Jo's hair was brown and did not glint in the sun, but it was still a very satisfying chestnut color.

"No," she said. "Did you spend your morning of not-so-quiet reflection thinking about how we're going to kick butt at—"

"Why, yes, in fact I did take a moment to reflect on that particular subject during my morning reflections, YES I DID!" April clenched her hands into tiny, powerful fists.

"I mean," she took a preparatory breath. "Of course we're going to rule the camp TO THE MAX at Galaxy Wars. Because we are awesome. And if there WERE a best cabin, which, let's say that most rankings of any sort are subjective, but that you could set a roughly scaled order using a few key components like who is most prepared and most learned, then the most amazing cabin would have to be US!"

Jo paused while April took a deep breath.

Winning was not really as interesting to Jo as many other things. It didn't even make her top-fifty things, if we're honest.

5

Winning was in April's top-ten interesting things. Currently under April's bunk was a stack of books on stars and planets. Under April's pillow was a dusty encyclopedia volume, *Me–Mo*, which covered subjects including medicine, merchants, monasteries, and, crucially, moons.

"I mean," April said, standing up straight again, "obviously, it's not about winning or losing, that's not what being a Lumberjane is about, and thus it's not what we're about, as Lumberjanes. Obviously it's about having fun, and we will have fun because that's what we do."

And then, April had a crystal-clear thought, and that thought was, *That, and WINNING.*

"Obviously," Jo agreed.

Admittedly, Jo was half listening to April and half thinking about the moon-like craft she thought she saw landing in the trees the other night from her window in the cabin. Jo had followed what for Jo was standard procedure after this sighting, which was to try and collect more information. Which meant jumping out of bed in the middle of the night with her flashlight and rooting through the bushes for an hour, discovering nothing but a wayward nest of squirrels who did not enjoy the intrusion.

Jo wondered if maybe it was a dream.

A very vivid, very awake-feeling dream.

This thought must have registered on Jo's face like a

flicker of light. Like a dragonfly skipping across the calm waters of a summer lake.

April squinted, noticing the flicker. "Hey," she said, and she was about to ask what WAS on Jo's mind, but then the mess hall door swung open, and they were swallowed up by the cacophony of breakfast.

CHAPTER 2

It is important to be VERY, VERY LOUD in the mess hall when you are a Lumberjane. It helps with digestion. If you cannot chew loudly and/or burp loudly, you can also slam your cutlery against the table and/or sing a song, of which, if you are a Lumberjane, there are many. Like that song about the GOAT, the GIRL, and the GARGOYLE playing GOLF. A song that is curiously titled, "Miss Maggy Marple May's Monday."

At the table, Ripley, the smallest but mightiest member of Roanoke cabin, was not singing but defending her pancake record of 14¾. A day earlier, Sally Smithereen of Roswell cabin (who had the record for most milkshakes slurped, at six) came very close to breaking it, except Sally made the rookie mistake of adding a bite of veggie bacon to the mix, and it all went south from there.

As it will.

The key to any record, as any Lumberjane knows, is focus. Which Ripley had, when it came to eating pancakes. When she wasn't eating pancakes, Ripley had a tendency to get distracted by sparkly things. Sparkly was one of Ripley's top-five favorite adjectives, along with fuzzy, bouncy, shiny, and googley.

In addition to eating breakfast, Mal and Molly, two particularly inseparable Roanoke cabin members, were practicing on their accordions for their upcoming That's Accordion to You badges. Successfully completing a badge for music meant performing for Drucilla Johnstone II, the ornery but lovable camp music director and master of multiple instruments, including the tuba, flute, drums, guitar, sitar, recorder, kazoo, harmonica, and violin. Drucilla avoided sunlight at all costs and thought disco was uniformly abominable, but she was a good teacher.

To receive badges, scouts had to play, for Drucilla, without mistakes, a song of their choosing, and three scales.

Music was definitely in Mal's list of favorite things, in addition to problem-solving and being really into Molly. Mal's mother and grandmother had been teaching her to play various instruments since she was old enough to breathe. One of her first stuffed animals was a fluffy drum named BANG.

Running her fingers over the buttons and keys of her accordion, Mal watched Molly, who was looking at her sheet music with great Molly-like intensity.

Before camp, music was not even in Molly's list of favorite one hundred things, although she enjoyed listening to the radio. Before camp, Molly had never even tried to play a musical instrument, but she was kind of digging playing music with Mal, mostly because just about anything she and Mal did together ended up being way more fun than anything Molly did with anyone else. Molly liked it so much she was even thinking of joining Flute Club.

Flute Club, unfortunately, was difficult to join, because they were a very secretive club. And no one really talks about how or where you're supposed to go to join.

Weird.

With Bubbles the raccoon, faithful pet and head warmer, snoozing comfortably on her noggin, Molly squinted at the notes on the page and tried to make her fingers go where they were supposed to go.

"What are you playing for your test tomorrow?" April asked. "Are you playing the classic Lumberjane ditty, 'Miss Tawny Tooberang Tustle's Tuesday'?"

"Is that the one about the hedgehog named Henry who hates horseradish?" Jo asked.

Molly shook her head. "I couldn't find any sheet music for that, so I'm playing 'Frère Jacques' instead." Molly braced her fingers on the keys of her accordion. "It's about a monk who slept in."

"I'm playing Queen's 'Bohemian Rhapsody,' " Mal said, "which is about relationships."

"Holy Siouxsie Sioux." April flopped down on the bench with a plate full of cheese omelette and toast. "Isn't that a really hard song?"

Mal shrugged. "Yeah, I mean, it's a suite containing a multitude of sections that is considered the ultimate hard-rock classical slash prog-rock crossover. No bigs."

"Dude," April nodded appreciatively. "Now that is an operatic undertaking!"

"It's gonna be athom," Ripley said, grinning with a mouth full of pancake.

Jo raised an eyebrow at Ripley. "Hey, Rip. How many pancakes is that?"

Ripley held up all ten sticky fingers.

People have a habit of saying odd and interesting things, like, "Your eyes were bigger than your stomach," which means you thought something was going to be smaller than it was, namely, that you thought a meal or a muffin or a buffet was going to be able to fit into your stomach, but it wasn't. Really, this is a way of saying that your stomach is smaller than you think, because no matter what you eat, your eyes stay pretty much the same size. Maybe it's not worth thinking about. Or maybe it's the key to everything.

Jo had spent a considerable amount of time wondering about whether or not Ripley had an extremely large stomach, or whether she was burning fuel at such a rapid Ripley rate while doing Ripley things that she just needed more fuel.

"Hey," Molly looked up. "Where's Jen?"

"Working on Galaxy Wars, of course," April said.

Galaxy Wars was Roanoke counselor extraordinaire Jen's pet project, if by "pet" we mean "obsession."

"Is it just me or has it been days since we saw her?" Mal wondered out loud. "She hasn't even bothered to leave us a list of chores in, like, three days. Or to tell us to be careful. I don't even know where my socks are anymore."

CLANG! CLANG! CLANG!

"LUMBERJANES! LISTEN UP!"

Camp Director Rosie, Jen, and the rest of the camp counselors stood at the front of the mess hall. Rosie, holding up a massive cast-iron pan and wooden spoon, was doing the clanging.

"LISTEN UP!" Rosie hollered, her voice piercing and loud like freshly sharpened steel.

The din subsided to a low murmur of chewing and curiosity.

Rosie lowered the pan and adjusted her thick cat-eye glasses. "RIGHT! Tonight will kick off our First Annual Lumberjane Galaxy Wars, organized by your very own camp counselors, including Roanoke's very own Jacqueline! Let's give her a hand!"

A roar of volcanic proportions erupted in the hall as all the scouts stood up to applaud their hardworking counselors.

"It's Jen," Jen whispered, clapping while keeping her trusty clipboard tucked under her arm. "Always Jen."

"YEAH, JEN!" Mal cheered.

"WOOT! WOOT!" Ripley yelled.

Jo just smiled, because Jo was less of a "WOOT"-er than her cabin mates.

Jen stepped forward, her counselor uniform crisp, smiling the rosy smile of a nerd about to see her dream take shape.

Jen had many dreams, including a recurring nightmare where she searched for her campers through a complex maze of thick ivy, all while dressed in a set of fuzzy footie pajamas and a baseball hat that said "HONK FOR JUSTICE."

This wasn't one of those dreams.

This was one of those dreams where you work really hard to make something happen, and then it does.

13

"All right, campers! We're all super excited to bring you this incredible event full of amazing . . . EVENTS!" Jen's eyes sparkled as she gazed out upon the crowd of campers about to take part in this amazing thing. This really amazing thing!

"Ahem," fellow counselor Vanessa nudged Jen, who in gazing had forgotten to mention . . . the events.

"Right!" Jen looked back down at her clipboard. "SO! Galaxy Wars will consist of four days of activities, all taking place after sunset. The first night, tonight, will be a camp-wide scavenger hunt. Tomorrow night we will have a mystery contest."

April's eyebrows shot up as high as a person's eyebrows could possibly shoot up.

Ripley sighed. "I hope it's a dance off. Bubbles and I have been practicing our cha-cha all week."

Bubbles, who was mostly Molly's pet but also Ripley's dance partner, chirped in the affirmative.

"The next day," Jen continued, "there will be a trivia contest with a distinctly Lumberjane twist!"

Mal hoped it wasn't anything to do with a lake. Or a river. Or water.

"And finally, the pièce de résistance, an all-out obstacle course!"

The mess hall erupted in a raucous cheer.

Lumberjanes love obstacles.

Because obstacles do not stand in the way of being an awesome scout.

Obstacles are what MAKE awesome scouts.

"The cabin that wins each event will receive twenty-five points; the second and third place cabins receive fifteen and ten points. The cabin with the most points at the end of four nights wins! The prize," Jen grinned, "will be announced at the first event tonight."

Jen held up a finger. "Get ready. These events are all night events, so bring your flashlights!"

"Okay, scouts," Vanessa hollered, "you've got the rest of your day to get to your tasks and responsibilities and badges. Zodiac, you have stable duty!"

With yips and yelps of glee, the scouts flooded out of the mess hall.

CHAPTER 3

Later that morning, Jo was walking from the metalsmithing workshop to the library when she spotted a cluster of bubbles wafting in the breeze.

Which is not a completely unexpected thing, but it was curious enough that Jo peeked behind the mess to see where the bubbles were coming from. She spotted BunBun sitting on the back steps.

BunBun was the daughter of Chef Kzzyzy Koo and a very interesting person. This summer, she had taken to wearing little cat ears. Cat ears, NOT bunny ears.

"Hey BunBun," Jo chirped.

"I'm very busy," BunBun said, very seriously, blowing on her little plastic wand and sending another flurry of bubbles into the breeze.

BunBun was always very busy doing whatever it was she was doing.

Last week Jo had spotted BunBun petting the grass. When her mother called her, BunBun called back, "I'm VERY BUSY!" Then she continued to pet the grass for another five minutes before wandering off to talk to a tree.

Behind the mess, coming from the kitchen, you could hear the boom of Janis Joplin and the high notes of Chef Kzzyzy Koo, roaring along with the music while pots and pans clanged, an orchestra of metal and lung. Kzzyzy Koo didn't cook without the freshest ingredients and a set list of music from the '60s. She grew her own veggies and herbs (pronounced with a hard "h" in this case), with the help of the scouts earning their Grow Up! badges.

It has been said that in a former life, Kzzyzy Koo was denied organic produce but toured the world as a drummer in one of several possible rock bands.

Now she was a chef who sang her way through prep with a throaty yowl you could hear across camp.

Jo stepped toward BunBun. "Nice bubbles," she said.

"I KNOW," BunBun said tersely.

Kzzyzy came out onto the back step, her waist-length blue hair tied into an impossibly big knot on the top of her head, her face flush from the heat of the ovens and the many pots and pans boiling and sizzling away inside. "Hey Jo!"

17

She waved, then, kneeling down, she looked at BunBun. "Hey. Have you been nibbling at the cheese, BunBun?"

BunBun frowned. "NO!"

"Sugary shortbread," Kzzyzy grumbled. Kzzyzy was wearing her KOO COOKS FOR YOO apron today, which was already stained with any number of sauces and spices. She put her hands on her hips. "How is it I'm missing like a pound of Alaskan Hybrid Goat Cheese?"

"That's a pretty big nibble," Jo noted.

"I don't E-VEN LIKE Alaskan HY-BRID Goat Cheese," BunBun announced in her carefully enunciated yells, waving her wand and sending up a cluster of bubbles. "I like CHE-DDAR, I like GOU-DA, and I like Himalayan Holey HA-VAR-TI."

Jo liked Parmesan, provolone, and pecorino. Preferably pasteurized.

Kzzyzy stood and scratched her head. "Then where did that Alaskan Hybrid go?"

In the distance, Jo spotted Rosie tromping through the grass with what looked like a massive net tossed over her shoulder.

BunBun followed Jo's gaze.

"There is a lot happening here all the time," she said to Jo.

"That's true," Jo said, assuming BunBun meant a lot of somewhat unexplainable things.

"And NOT all of it is about CHEESE," BunBun insisted.

"It's only ever some of the time about cheese," Jo agreed.

Seemingly from thin air, BunBun pulled out a small briefcase. She tapped her ears and stood up, some leftover bubbles still buzzing in the air.

"I have to go," she said to Jo. "I have a big meeting. I'm VERY busy."

Jo watched BunBun toddle off before realizing she had stuff to do too.

Hmmm, Jo thought to herself. *Cheese.*

CHAPTER 4

The First Annual Lumberjanes Official Opening Ceremony for the First Annual Lumberjane Galaxy Wars took place at an hour that old people who like to walk on the beach call "The Magic Hour."

(Which is just on the edge of sunset.)

Scouts were inside the mess hall finishing dinner when there was a sudden *CLANG! CLANG! CLANG! CLANG!*

Ripley jumped up, almost losing the scoop from her ice cream cone. "HOLY CARRIE FISHER, IT'S TIME!"

Bubbles hovered by Ripley's elbow as she ran outside, ready to catch a frosty nibble.

April grabbed Jo's sleeve. "Come on!!"

Everyone burst out into the courtyard . . . to encounter another world.

Ripley let out an exhilarated breath.

"WHOOOOOA!"

Suffice it to say, Jen and the rest of the counselors of Miss Qiunzella Thiskwin Penniquiqul Thistle Crumpet's camp for Hardcore Lady-Types had truly outdone themselves.

Which is sort of typical for Lumberjanes. Why just "do," when "out-doing" is so much better?

The front of the mess hall was covered in an arcade of twinkling lights. The ground was covered in a galaxy of constellations painted with nontoxic paints. Strings of different-colored bulbs circled the camp, flickering pink and blue and white. Fireflies, unaware they were part of the show, zoomed down and around.

"It's like floating in a sea of stars," Molly marveled, holding her arms out as she slowly spun around to take it all in. "Space without the inconvenience of space travel."

It reminded Jo of sitting in the planetarium with her dads when she was little.

Each cabin had a small flag behind which stood a gaggle of excited, anticipating scouts.

The members of Zodiac cabin—Barney, Emily, Hes, Wren, and Skulls—pulled little star bands out of their pockets and strapped them to their heads. They looked tough. Like a solar army. They looked ready for solar battle.

"Zodiac look rad," Ripley said, waving at Barney, who waved back jubilantly, their silver star twinkling against their raven-colored hair.

"We should have a star thing too," Molly added.

"Ooo!" Mal reached up and gave Bubbles a pet. "Or we could make Bubbles our team mascot."

Molly looked up at Bubbles, who was licking ice cream off his little raccoon lips. "Maybe we could make him a little moon hat or something."

Rosie stepped up to the platform next to the flag-pole, wearing a pair of star-shaped glasses instead of her usual cat-eye rims. She addressed the crowd of wide-eyed scouts.

"WELCOME, LUMBERJANES! CABINS! IF YOU HAVEN'T ALREADY, PLEASE FIND YOUR FLAG AND STAND BEHIND IT!"

Roanoke clustered next to their flag, which to Ripley's delight was the same color of blue as the streak in her hair.

Rosie held up her hand. "As you all know, this is our First Annual Lumberjane Galaxy Wars event, and your counselors and I have spent considerable time deciding what reward should go to the winning cabin."

April rubbed her hands together.

"The winning team will have their names engraved on the first-ever GALAXY WARS CUP, and their portrait will hang in the Mess for the rest of the summer."

"Great Lady Dana Deveroe," Mal whistled, recalling the former Lumberjane who now lived in the clouds and was obsessed with winning things and having people remember her for winning things.

"In addition," Rosie opened her hand to reveal a shining silver pin in the shape of a comet, "each cabin member will receive a Celestial Shield!"

"Twiiiinkly," Ripley oooooed.

The rest of the scouts ahhhhhh-ed appropriately.

"WE are getting that shield," Hes hissed to her fellow Zodiacs.

April looked over at Zodiac. Her competition. Then she looked at the shield again. *That's what you think*, she thought.

Jo looked at the sky and thought about the fact that the stars we see up in the sky, from Earth, are actually stars that might have gone out decades ago, which makes them sort of space ghosts. If there are space ghosts, Jo wondered, what else could be up there?

"Hey," April grinned as she poked her elbow into Jo's side. "This is no time to SPACE out!"

Jo rolled her eyes. "Let the space puns begin."

Rosie tucked the Celestial Shield back into her pocket. "Best of luck, scouts!"

CHAPTER 5

Someone pressed PLAY somewhere, and heavenly strains of Tasmin Archer filled the camp. The door to the mess hall creaked open, releasing a dramatic cloud of pink smoke.

As the smoke trickled down the steps and over the stars painted on the ground, a line of Lumberjane camp counselors appeared through the mist in fishbowl helmets and silver gloves.

"Holy Sally Ride." Molly pressed her hands to her face.

The music faded, and one astronaut stepped forward and removed her helmet to reveal . . . JEN!

"Yeah, Jen!" Ripley cheered. "ASTRONAUT POWER!"

Jen smiled as she raised her intergalactic megaphone to her lips. "LUMBERJANE SCOUTS! ON BEHALF

OF THE LEAGUE OF GALAXY, I PRESENT THE CELESTIAL SCAVENGER HUNT!"

What is a celestial scavenger hunt and why is it so exciting?

Well, first of all, just about any scavenger hunt, which is a hunt for things using clues, is exciting. A scavenger hunt takes that classic question, "Where is it?" and poses another question: "I don't know, why don't you use your brain and go find it?"

A Lumberjane scavenger hunt is not your average scavenge. In the early, early, EARLY days, the Lumberjanes held scavenger hunts that lasted three days and three nights, long after anyone could even remember what it was they were looking for.

"SCOUTS! You must use your skills and knowledge of astronomy—and scouts who have their Astrono-me-me-me badges will definitely have an advantage—to find eight orbs, one orb for each of the eight planets, which I and your fellow counselors have hidden all over camp!"

The members of Roanoke, all of whom had the Astrono-me-me-me badge, grinned.

Obviously. I mean, when you have Jen the astrono-obsessed as your camp counselor, you learn a little something about the stars and planets.

"The game ends when all of the orbs are found. The

27

cabin with the most orbs WINS!" Jen announced. She could not stop smiling. I mean come on, planets, stars, and guided activities for campers? What could be better?

"OKAY," Vanessa called out as she stepped up with a bullhorn.

"SCOUTS, GET READY!"

"On your MADELEINE."

"Get SAMARA!"

"GUADALUPE!"

TWOOOOOOOOONK!

They're off!

"GRACE HOPPER FORMATION!" April shouted, pointing up at the sky in a dramatic pose worthy of the occasion. The scouts shifted into two lines.

"All right scouts," April said, putting her hands on Jo's and Ripley's shoulders and leaning in conspiratorially, "tonight is the first night of our momentous celestial victory, our first step toward planetary greatness."

"Okay," Molly said.

"First things first," April said, pulling out a pen, "let's make a list of all the planets, which is ULTIMATELY a list of all the orbs we will find on our path to victory."

"Right. Mercury," Mal said, starting to count them off on her fingers.

"Venus," April added.

"Earth!" Ripley cheered. "Mars! Jupiter! Saturn!"

"Uranus and Neptune," Jo said.

Mercury

Venus

Earth

Mars

Jupiter

Saturn

Uranus

Neptune

April looked at her arm. "So we know that each planet's facts are the clues to where they're hidden. So that could be the name of the planet . . ."

"It could have something to do with the temperature of the planets," Mal added.

"Or the atmosphere," Ripley gasped. "Or the color."

"Or it could be relative to where they are to the sun," Jo said, picturing a map of camp and several circles representing the various orbits of the planets around the sun.

"Or their names," Mal noted.

Jo mentally flipped open her dog-eared copy of *Everything You Wanted to Know About Roman Mythology and Then Some*.

Just then Molly's face lit up like a light bulb, or a star. "I've got it!"

29

CHAPTER 6

What's in a name? Technically your name is something someone gives you when you are born, which means your name is something someone who's just met you, in the flesh, gives you, on the first day you exist.

April was named for a month her mother liked.

Mal was named after a character in an '80s sitcom that her mom thought was really funny.

Molly was named after her great-grandmother.

Ripley was named Ripley because of her father's favorite alien movie.

Jo was the only person in her cabin who had chosen her name. She'd chosen her new name when she was ten. She liked that it took only two letters to spell, which made her think of the periodic table.

Planets are also named, not by parents but by the people who first spotted them in the sky and thought, "Hey, I think that's a planet." In most cases these people were Romans. This is probably why the planets are named mostly after Greek and Roman gods.

(It's a true, but weird, story that the planet Uranus was almost named Herschel, possibly because of the astronomer William Herschel, who discovered Uranus, although he'd wanted to name it George's Star, after King George III.

Totally true.

It would be kind of cool to have a planet named Herschel though, don't you think? Or George? Or Cathy. Cathy would be nice.

Not coincidentally, when Jo was little she had a toy microscope named Herschel the Microscope.)

"Mercury," Molly huffed, as she led Roanoke scrambling across camp, "is named after Mercury the messenger, right?"

"Correct," April puffed, speeding up.

"So what's a place associated with messages?" Molly asked.

"The mail room?" April asked.

"There is no mail room anymore," Jo noted.

31

The mail room had been invaded by a band of marauding squirrels looking for cookies several years ago, and now the mail room was just a sack Rosie kept locked in her office.

All the members of Roanoke cabin suddenly flashed on the same image.

April snapped her fingers. "EUREKA!"

Mal grinned at Molly. "You're so smart," she gushed.

Jo nodded.

Ripley jumped up in mid-run.

"The phone booth!" they all whispered, so as not to let the rest of the cabins, whizzing around, know their plan.

The phone booth wasn't actually a working phone booth, because most phone booths now are historical relics people point out and say, "Aw, look, a phone booth." This booth even had a phone with a rotary dial, which you can also chalk up to a thing of nostalgia (which is when people miss things that aren't around anymore). The booth was very much like a small wooden cabin, with no real purpose or explanation for being. Why a phone booth in the woods? There was a rumor that there was a secret number you could dial on the phone that would send the booth into another dimension, but April hadn't figured it out yet.

Not for lack of trying, mind you.

Picking up the pace, the members of Roanoke cabin charged past the library and hooked around the stables to where the phone booth was semi-hidden, tucked in amongst a thicket of pine trees.

"HARK!!" April cried, pointing through the trees. "OVER THERE!"

It was Zodiac, who had obviously had the same idea and were running toward the booth from the other side of the stables.

April gritted her teeth. Zodiac were picking up speed!

The members of Zodiac were many things, and, unfortunately, in this moment, fast was one of them. Hes and Emily were both the stars of their basketball teams back home, and now the whole cabin was pounding through the trees with their eyes fixed on a slam-dunk.

Jo had another idea. "Hey, Rip!" She lowered her hands in a loop. "ROCKET RIPLEY TIME?"

Ripley grinned a mischievous grin. "YAAAS!"

And with that, Ripley sped up, jumped, put one foot on Jo's hands, and was hoisted with all of Jo's might into the air with the speed of a comet, cutting through space, hurtling toward its intended target.

"ROOOCKKKEEET RIIIIIIPLLLEEEEEY!"

April shielded her eyes. "Going."

Mal squinted at disappearing Ripley. "Going!"

Jo, of course, had mentally mapped Ripley's likely trajectory, considering Ripley's average speed, weight, height, and general Ripley-ness.

"Three," Jo whispered, "two . . ."

Molly smiled. "Aaaaaaanddd . . ."

RIPLEY ZOOOOM!

Ripley landed on a patch of pine needles and bounced up onto her feet a few steps from the booth. She tucked and rolled, stood, and dove through the doors of the booth. There it was, glowing like a radical orange sonic jewel on top of the receiver.

"I GOT IT!" Ripley cried, hopping on top of the booth and holding up the orb with one hand.

MERCURY!

CHAPTER 7

The camp was chaos: flashlights bobbing in the dark and voices calling out "OVER HERE!" and "OVER WHERE?!" and "OVER *HERE!*"

Owls sitting on their perches hooted and tipped their heads at impossible angles, annoyed because making weird noises at night was *their* thing.

The counselors, still in their helmets, peered out from behind trees and from rooftops as the rest of the scouts foraged their brains for a hint as to where the planets might be hidden.

Zodiac beat Roanoke to the next orb, Saturn, which was tucked in next to the wool-crafting area in the arts and crafts cabin. Because Saturn, as owners of the Astrono-me-me-me as well as the Wool You Be Mine badge know, has shepherd moons.

Shepherds → Sheep → Wool.

Kind of a stretch but, you know, okay.

"Garr," April fumed as they tromped away from arts and crafts, the cheers of Zodiac cabin melting into the dark behind them.

"At least we guessed the right place," Molly offered hopefully.

"These clues are . . . curious," Jo said.

Molly blinked, looking into the darkness. It was strange, she thought, how the dark was like its own thing to see, a whole extra world of shadows and shapes.

"What we need," April said, pointing her flashlight at her own determined face, "is a super-amazing PLAN-et."

"HEY!" Mal snapped her fingers. "Isn't Mars the god of war?"

"Amongst other things," noted April, who had done her research.

"What's the closest thing we have to weapons here?"

Molly squinted. "Are you thinking archery?"

Mal smiled. "I'm very much thinking archery."

April raised an eyebrow at their mind-reading. This was a new couple-y thing.

"The archery targets are all the way on the other side of camp," Jo said, taking off at a sprint.

"We can make it!" Molly knew the archery section of camp well, since discovering she was actually a pretty crack shot, something she never would have guessed about herself before becoming a Lumberjane.

Several minutes of sprinting later, April spotted their targets.

"I see it," she squealed excitedly, reaching out to the glowing orb in the distance. "Come to me, you great glowing orb of triumph."

Mal, in mid-run, looked over her shoulder. "Do you hear that?"

April's eyes widened. "Did I just say all that out loud?"

Mal shook her head. "Not that. THAT!"

Everyone skidded to a stop.

Actually what Mal heard was several sounds: breaking branches. A thunderous *thump thump thump*. And a distinct, victorious yipping.

Jo frowned. "What the junk."

With a glorious flash, the members of Zodiac, astride a massive majestic moose, leapt over the crouching members of Roanoke and gregariously galloped toward the targets, where Hes, balancing on her moose's massive curved horns, reached down and plucked the glowing red orb from a set of crossed arrows embedded in the center of the target.

"WOOOT! WOOOOT!" Zodiac cheered collectively.

37

"THE ORB IS OURS!" Hes cheered.

"YAAAAS!" Wren cried.

And with that, Zodiac galloped off into the night.

"What the actual JUNK!" April growled, shaking her fists.

"Now *that* stings," Molly added.

Bubbles growled.

"Exactly," Jo said.

"COME ON! MOOSE POWER?!" April fumed. "They're using MOOSE POWER now?! Is that even a thing?! Can you just randomly call upon the power of MOOSE just like that?"

"I don't think there's a rule that says you can't use moose power," Jo mused, knowing full well that there probably wasn't, although there were a lot of rules for being a Lumberjane, most of which Jo knew, because that was kind of her thing.

There was a *yip yipping* from over by the kitchen, where Roswell found Earth in the garden. Because EARTH.

"Not aMOOSing," April said, arms crossed crossly.

Jo tapped her chin. "So that's two planets for Zodiac, one for us and . . . from the sounds of it, one for Roswell."

"All right, Lumberjanes." April stood up. "We're in the thick of it now. Mooses on the left, unfound planets on the right . . ."

39

April clenched her fist and bowed her head slightly. "Now is a time for greatness . . . Now is the time for . . . PLANET B."

Jo smiled. "Well punned my friend."

April, fist still clenched, grinned. "I have SOOOOOO many planet puns left, you guys."

CHAPTER 8

There was a rustling in the trees. An astronaut seemingly floated into the thicket to inform them, in a muffled, inside-a-fishbowl voice, that three other planets had been located.

Uranus, aka Herschel, was tucked into the tire swing hanging out behind Rosie's cabin. Obviously someone in Woolpit, possibly Maxine P., remembered that Uranus is the only planet that spins up on its side.

Dartmoor found Jupiter, the largest of the planets, by the lake, possibly because Jupiter has the largest ocean in the solar system, although, as Jo pointed out, its ocean consisted mostly of helium and hydrogen.

The scouts of Dighton found Neptune in the ice box next to a stack of popsicles and a very large tub of frozen peanut butter (which was probably not part of the competition).

"Is it me," Mal asked, "or are these some weird connections?"

"Well, it's a lot of planets, and a lot of clues to figure out," Molly said. "I'd give whoever had to make them up a break."

"One planet left," the astronaut said. "Get on it, scouts."

"Come on, guys." April slammed her fist into her open palm. "Are we SCOUTS? Or are we MICE?"

"We're scouts," Ripley said, "but mice are nice too."

"Look!" Jo said, holding up her flashlight like a torch. "The only planet left is VENUS. Let's all think really really hard about where that would be."

Everyone thought. Very, very hard.

In mid Jo-think, Jo heard what she thought was a swishing sound over her left shoulder. Much smaller than a moose. She spun around to catch a glimpse of a flash of light darting between the trees. Like a flashlight but softer. Like a glow. Was it one of the counselors?

She swiveled her flashlight in the direction of the noise but all she got was a hole in the dark.

"Okay, idea," Mal declared. "And I know how we can get there without anyone spotting us."

"Creep across the ground like caterpillars?" Ripley offered. "Dig a tunnel?"

"Nope." Mal held up her flashlight and—click—turned it off. "They can't *see* us if they can't see us."

"Stealth mode!" April whispered excitedly.

"How are we not going to bump into trees?" Molly asked.

"Ooo," Mal looked at her flashlight. "Good question."

"If only we had a night vision magic kitty," Ripley mused.

Night vision magic kitties, while a pain in the butt to have around when you're trying to sleep, are incredibly useful things in the dark. Laser kitties, same thing.

"Oh!" Jo raised a finger and pointed it at Molly's head. "But we do!"

"BUBBLES!" Ripley cheered.

"Raccoons have excellent night vision," Jo noted. "And Bubbles knows his way around camp."

Molly had used Bubbles for fetching supplies in past dinosaur emergencies, but not in the middle of the night.

Molly reached up and plucked the chirping Bubbles off her head. "Hey, buddy," she whispered, "can you do us a little favor?"

Bubbles chirped an affirmative, and Mal told him where they needed to go.

In conga line formation, with Bubbles in the lead, the members of Roanoke cabin headed to what Mal figured out to be the hiding place of the last planet.

43

"The infirmary," Ripley whispered, when they got closer.

"Of course," April cheered . . . quietly.

Jo thought, but did not say, that it looked like they were the only ones to think of this spot for the last planet. (Jo was not a fan of saying things that just about anyone could look around and see were true. Oh, if only more people were like Jo.)

There were a lot of places the counselors could have hidden the planet associated with the goddess of love: the tennis courts, since "love" is a score in tennis. There was also a tree just past Jo's favorite turtle-shaped rock stuffed with love letters, although only two scouts knew about that.

It was Vanessa, counselor for Zodiac, famous for her cast-iron hair spikes, who chose the defibrillator, a machine used to restart hearts, in part because it had an actual heart painted on the side.

"At least some of these planet clues," Vanessa argued, "should be a LITTLE BIT obvious."

Jen thought all the clues were obvious.

The orb representing Venus was painted to look like cracked amber.

Mal and Molly both reached for it at the same time. Both stepped back and smiled shyly.

"You take it," Mal offered, blushing.

"No, it's okay," Molly smiled, "you grab it."

"Nah, it's cool, you take it."

"We could grab it together," Molly whispered.

"GOT IT!" Ripley appeared in the middle, snatching the orb. "YOINK!"

Ripley had only just tucked the glowing orange orb into her pocket when there was a loud clanging.

Astronaut camp counselors ran through the camp calling

out, "ALL THE PLANETS HAVE BEEN COLLECTED! ALL CABINS MUST NOW CONGREGATE AT THE LOCATION IN CAMP REPRESENTING THE SUN!"

"The sun is . . . hot!" Ripley said.

"It's at the center of *this* solar system," Jo added.

"The mess hall," April said. "The oven in the mess hall!"

Outside the infirmary, the camp rumbled with the sound of many scout feet running toward the mess hall, pushing past trees and charging down the paths that led to the starry start of this whole thing, scouts whooping and hollering, their flashlights bobbing in the dark.

Just before the steps of the mess hall, Bubbles, who had been running alongside Molly, stopped and sniffed the air, curious.

"Come on, Bubbs!" Ripley called out, as she took the steps of the mess hall two by two.

Bubbles made a little clicking sound, like a nervous clock.

"What is it, Bubbs?" Jo asked, crouching next to him and peering into the dark. "You see something?"

Bubbles sniffed the night air.

"COME ON!" Mal called from the top of the steps.

Molly scooped up Bubbles and popped him onto her head.

Everyone clambered up the steps to the mess hall where Kzzyzy Koo, wearing a silver suit, and BunBun, in a green alien jumpsuit, waited along with the counselors.

"WELCOME TO THE PIZZA PARTY AT THE CENTER OF THE UNIVERSE!" Kzzyzy hollered.

With that, Kzzyzy stepped aside to reveal a giant sun-shaped pizza pie, fresh out of the oven, set up on the table.

Holding up her clipboard, Jen waited until the pizza cheer died down.

"CONGRATULATIONS TO ALL ON A SCAVEN-GER HUNT WELL SCAVENGED! And special congratulations to ROANOKE and ZODIAC for taking the lead with two orbs each. And three cheers to ALL the scouts who used their wits to find some well-hidden planets tonight!"

Hip hip!

"HOORAY!"

"TIED!" April shouted, looking at Jo with a look Jo interpreted as pleased but also incredibly determined to do better next time.

"And now," Rosie declared, "A night of good hunting deserves a re—"

"Hey!" BunBun cried out, pointing at the pizza. "LOOK!"

The pizza, decorated with every possible topping, including healthy gobs of mozzarella, was missing a huge bite out of the side.

"AW, COME ON!" Kzzyzy growled. "Seriously? What the Mary Berry is going on here?!"

47

The bite was about the size of a salad plate.

"Hmmm," Rosie said, as she peered. "Well at least we know it's not a Karactopod."

Barney, a member of Zodiac and a very well-read Lumberjane, stepped forward out of the crowd. "It's not a big bite," they observed, looking closely. "It's lots and lots of little bites. Which means it was probably something small. These bite marks look almost . . ."

Jo peered over Barney's shoulder. "Rodent?"

Barney nodded.

"All right!" Kzzyzy stormed into the kitchen, "it's moon PB and J for everyone. Hold your horses."

Mal looked at Molly looked at Ripley looked at April looked at Jo.

"Something in this camp likes cheese," Jo said quietly. "A lot."

CHAPTER 9

By the next morning, the mystery of the missing pizza was washed away by the many many many other things that Lumberjanes have to think about on an average day.

Which for Molly—sitting outside Drucilla Johnstone II's music studio, a black box with no windows and a curiously skinny front door—were the notes:

C – D – E – C – C – D – E – C

"I've never taken a music test before," Molly said, balancing her accordion on her right knee while her left knee shook with nerves.

Molly had never really liked tests. Molly had many nightmares about pencils breaking while she was taking a test. Once she had a dream where she was supposed to take a test but her only pencil was eight feet long and didn't have an eraser.

Mal, with her accordion strapped to her chest, shoved playfully into Molly. "You'll be great! Easy peasy!"

"I can't believe you chose such a hard song," Molly said. "I have like twelve notes and I'm freaking out! You have, like, a thousand notes."

"It's not THAT hard," Mal said, chill. "At home I learn a new song every week."

Inside the music studio, someone was trying for the Guitar It On badge with a plunky rendition of "Chelsea Morning."

"What if I mess it up?" Molly wondered aloud.

"First of all," Mal said with a soft smile, "you're not going to mess up. Just think of something nice in your head."

"Second of all," Mal looped her arm around Molly's shoulder and gave her a squeeze. "Even if you DO mess up, you're still awesome."

"Thanks," Molly said, her cheeks getting pink.

At last there was a pause and a scooting of chairs. "Okay." Mal pressed her forehead against Molly's. "You can do this."

Just around the corner, Jo was heading back to the cabin when she came across Rosie, who now, instead of a giant net, carried a brown sack labeled MAIL.

Of all of Rosie's tasks as camp director, getting mail was the one she was most likely to describe as a "royal A-1 Megalosaurus pain in the tush."

Very few people at camp knew who carried the mail from the outside world to camp, or could imagine the complexities involved in this task, which recently had gotten the better of Herman Opal Fluffy, the last mail carrier. Herman quit shortly after he was found up a tree in the woods just outside camp, looking white as a sheet, chanting, "SO many teeth. Such big eyes."

Fortunately, the new mail carrier HAD lots of teeth and big eyes, which Rosie was sincerely hoping would remedy the situation.

"Good morning, Jo," Rosie said with a quick nod as she passed.

"Good morning, Rosie!" Jo replied.

Rosie was about to charge off into the distance when she snapped her fingers.

"Oh! Jo!" She plonked the sack onto the ground, reached in, and pulled out a large, thick white envelope. So white it flashed in the sun. She handed it to Jo. "I almost forgot! This arrived for you."

Jo flipped the letter over in her hands. The envelope had a fancy crest for a return address. It was forwarded from Jo's home by her dads, who had scrawled the camp address over the original label in their cryptic scratch that even she found hard to read.

"Looks official," Rosie said, slinging her bag over her shoulder again. "Have a productive day!"

And Rosie disappeared off to wherever it is people like Rosie disappear to, as they do frequently, with bags and bunches and buckets of things.

Jo looked down at the letter in her hands.

The sensation was not unlike standing on a distant lunar surface, alone and jarringly, suddenly, out of orbit.

CHAPTER 10

One of the most important messages ever received by a Lumberjane arrived by post after many moons' journey.

It was a scroll, sealed with poppy-red beeswax and written in squid ink, which read:

World is not flat. World is round. Adjust plans accordingly.

For Jo, the letter she held in her hands felt similarly life changing.

Sitting on a rock in the middle of the woods, Jo stared at the text, wide eyed.

The Center for Scientific Advancement and Research is pleased to offer you an exclusive position in our Summer Theory and Advanced Astronomical Research Program, effective immediately.

Jo's fingers started to sweat, leaving little circle smears on the very thick letterhead.

"I didn't apply for a Summer Theory and Advanced Astronomical Research Program," Jo said, out loud, to the letter.

Admission to this program was based on your record of overall exemplary merit and achievement in the fields of mechanical engineering, quantum physics, and your recent first place in the "Reinvent the Wheel" Academic Olympics. It did not require an application.

"Oh," Jo said.

It sounded like kind of a big opportunity.

This is actually a once-in-a-lifetime incredible opportunity, the letter confirmed.

Jo looked at the letter again.

"Holy Maryam Mirzakhani," Jo gasped.

The program was being led by Professor Ellis Watters Stevenson Allen III.

That is correct.

Jo bit her lip. Professor Ellis Watters Stevenson Allen III produced some of the most dynamic theorems on space travel ever conceived. Two of her theories were published when she was seventeen years old.

Technically sixteen and a half, the letter added, somewhat smugly. I mean, if you want to get technical about it.

Working with someone like that could change your whole career. This kind of opportunity . . .

Could be life changing, the letter noted.

"Wait," Jo asked, rescanning the top paragraph. "The program starts immediately?"

Admission to the program would require students to appear at the institute no later than . . .

In one week. That was very very very soon.

Jo had always imagined that someday she would do something like this—that she would work with famous scientists, that she could BE a famous scientist.

Both of her dads studied at the Center for Scientific Advancement and Research before going on to study at various other centers in various other programs.

Eventually, Jo knew, this kind of opportunity would come knocking.

And now, the letter said, here I am.

"Hey!" Ripley stepped out of the trees. "What are you doing?"

"Oh." Jo stuffed the letter into one of her many coat pockets. "Nothing."

"Okay, um." Ripley stepped one sneaker on her other sneaker and twisted her arms behind her back. "I was hanging out with Barney but now Barney has to go help Zodiac with the cabin contest."

"Cabin contest?" Jo looked up and noticed for the first time that it was near dusk. Sky violet.

Jo jumped off the rock, her April sensors tingling. "Ohmygosh Rip! We gotta go!"

Grabbing hands, the two of them burst into a run.

CHAPTER 11

Jo arrived back at Roanoke just in time for a fit of pure Roanoke madness. Piled up in front of the cabin was a mess of materials, half of which, for a change, seemed to be twisted around Molly instead of Ripley.

April was doing her best to calmly and coolly organize a plan.

It was not going well.

"Neptune is cold, right?" she said, pacing in furious circles. "So we could do, what, icicles? What if we made snowflakes? Is that too obvious? Is obvious BAD?"

"Hey!" Jo said, skidding to a stop next to the cabin and the chaos with Ripley.

"What the LOUISE FITZHUGH?!" April frowned, still pacing. "Where have you been?"

"In the woods with Barney," Ripley reported with a very official tone.

Jo looked at Ripley. "Uh, me too. In the woods." She smiled nervously at April. "But I'm here now. What's happening?"

April pointed at the piece of paper BunBun had handed her. "Well we got our planet for the COSMIC CABIN CONTEST!"

"And we have NEPTUNE!" April continued. "Which, FIRST OF ALL, absolutely has to be the hardest planet to do for a decorating contest. SECOND OF ALL, we have an hour to figure out what we're going to do to decorate our cabin and no one has any ideas. THIRD OF ALL . . ."

"Third of all?" Jo asked.

"Okay, admittedly, it's just those two things," April admitted. "BUT IT IS A LOT AND I AM FREAKING OUT!"

"We have string," Molly said, uncoiling the many ribbons that had somehow mummied her arms while she was carrying them.

Jo looked up. Holy kittens it was getting late.

Mal opened her mouth to say something. Because normally, Mal was full of ideas.

Except.

Mal's mouth hung open. Silent.

Molly, still unstringing the ribbons from around her arm, raised an eyebrow. "You okay, Mal?"

Mal shrugged.

Jo stared blankly at the cabin. "Uh," she said. "Well. Okay."

It was like Jo's brain was trying to start an equation but all she could hear was the letter in her pocket.

Ahem. Quick reminder. Huge opportunity. In your pocket. Right now.

"There're winds on Neptune," April said, mostly to herself, pacing in circles of increasing circumference. "Aren't there? Can we use that? Can we make wind out of string? Is that weird? That's weird, right? It seems weird. Is it weird? Is that okay?"

"I think weird is okay," Molly offered.

April looked at Jo. April could not hear what Jo was hearing, but she could see Jo's face. Jo was clearly lost in thought, a place April knew Jo spent a lot of time. But there was something else. April couldn't quite decipher what it was.

"Jo?" April reached up and touched Jo's hand. "Are you okay?"

"Huh." Jo swung her head around to look at April. "What? Neptune? Right. Neptune."

The good thing about ideas is, if you don't have one, PROBABLY someone else has one you can borrow.

That's one of the great things about friends.

How smart they are.

Ripley suddenly remembered the haunted house she made with her family, which included a creepy howling wind that blew through their very crowded house.

"I KNOW I KNOW I KNOW!" Ripley said, waving her hand in the air to get everyone's attention. "I have an awesome idea! But Jo has to build something first."

CHAPTER 12

The cabin-judging committee consisted of Camp Director Rosie, Cook Kzzyzy Koo, and Seafarin' Karen, the marine instructor with a penchant for taking notes and keeping a clean ship.

Who was also a shapeshifter.

Which didn't affect her judging, but it seems pertinent to mention because the universe is a wonderful place full of people with abilities and skills you don't expect.

The sky was an umbrella of icy stars as the judges, clipboards in hand, walked through the carnival of decorated cabins.

Possibly you are thinking, *Hey, aren't Lumberjanes hearty adventurers who like to climb mountains and swing from vines and build fires from scratch?*

Uh YAH.

MANY are.

But this does not mean that Lumberjanes aren't also crafty as all get out.

A Lumberjane knows a slip stitch, a lanyard, a pipe cleaner triple twist, and can sequin the house DOWN.

Lumberjanes are so well rounded as a bunch they even have a See You a Well-Rounded badge, where scouts are encouraged to complete at least three different badges from three different disciplines and backgrounds.

Jo received this badge after taking up rug hooking (Off the Hook badge), Baseball (HEY BATTA BATTA! badge), and Haiku (575 badge).

Many bottles of glue and tubs of sparkles and boxes of pipe cleaners later, the cabins were ready to have their cabins judged.

Roswell cabin had Saturn, and they had built actual tracks of rings circling the cabin with little moon trains chugging along the tracks.

"These scouts came to PLAY," Kzzyzy marveled, her eyes alight.

"It's a steam train," Tabby, of Roswell, explained.

CHOO! CHOO!

Outside Zodiac, the judges were met by a committee of Zodiacs, all dressed in armor.

"Welcome to MARS!" Mackenzie, a.k.a. Skulls, announced. "The planet named after the god of war!"

Hes struck a match and touched it to the ground.

Instantly there was a shower of red sparks that lit up the cabin with a fury of red light.

Barney stood guard in their armor, a massive fire extinguisher in hand. "Safety first," they chirped.

"Marvelous," Rosie said, scribbling on her board.

"I like the safety touch," Kzzyzy added, nodding at Barney.

Barney had recently received their Better Safety Than

Sorry badge, for which they had to learn at least a dozen ways of preventing at least a dozen possible hazards (a badge that curiously did not include instructions for unplugging everything in the house before you leave to prevent fires).

"Arrrrg, not bad," Seafarin' Karen noted.

Zodiac high-fived.

"It's in the BAG," Wren said.

The judges turned and cast their eyes on their charts.

"The next cabin is . . . Roanoke," Kzzyzy said.

Rosie looked up and smiled. "Well, look at that!"

You could see Roanoke from a hundred steps away. Heck, you could probably see it from space.

It. Glowed.

A deep, ominous blue.

Like the dark heart of the ocean, but in space. Thanks to a bucket of phosphorescent paint mixed up by Molly, the entire cabin was painted in glowing stripes of blues and purples.

"Now that," Jen commented quietly to herself from her impartial corner with the rest of the counselors, "is not going to wash off."

On closer inspection, the planet of Neptune as created by Roanoke was also experiencing a perpetual windstorm, powered by a wind bicycle put together by Jo (based on Ripley's idea) using an old exercise bike, many elastic bands, and some folded paper fans. As April pedaled, the bike turned the fans, which in turn made a current of air that made the strings Ripley had taped to the roof and walls of the cabin dance wildly.

It's difficult to explain, but the effect was really cool.

On the roof, Ripley and Bubbles, dressed in a wild concoction of string and pipe cleaners and thoroughly drenched in phosphorescent paint, wriggled and whipped around like aliens tumbling in a Neptunian hurricane.

(If you looked closely, you might think it looked a bit like a cha-cha with an extra two or three wriggles added for good measure.)

"Welcome," Molly, Jo, and Mal, who were also painted blue, greeted the judges.

"This is Neptune, the icy windswept hurricane that is our solar system's most remote planet," Molly said.

"Very impressive," Seafarin' Karen said, looking down at her notes.

"It's very . . . creative!" Rosie smiled, making a note on her clipboard.

Seafarin' Karin saluted the scouts with a grin. "Nice blue, scouts."

"Next—" Rosie looked down at her list.

As the judges stepped away, Mal sighed and dropped down to the grass.

"Seriously," Molly frowned, sitting down next to her. "Are you okay?"

Mal touched her two index fingers together, tapping them

nervously. "Earlier. In the music portable? I didn't pass my test. I made too many mistakes so I didn't pass my badge."

"Aw!" Molly put a gentle hand on Mal's shoulder. "That's all right! It's like you said, just because you don't do something perfectly doesn't mean you're not still awesome."

"It's not the same," Mal said quietly, rubbing the back of her neck. "It's not the same for me. It's *music*."

"And?" Molly asked, tipping her head to the side.

"I'm the music person!" Mal burst, throwing out her arms. "You're the super cute and smart and supportive one with archery skills."

"Well," Molly said. "I don't—"

Mal pointed at April, who was staring intently at the cabin with her finger on her chin. "April is the feisty redhead with winning drive. Jo is the smart one with the even temperament. Ripley is the speeding bullet with the blue hair and the love of animals."

Mal pressed her hands to her chest. "And I'M the musical one with the cool hair and clothes!"

"What's going on?" Jo wandered over, scratching her nose because DayGlo paint is really itchy.

"I didn't pass my badge," Mal grumbled, getting to her feet.

"Well, can you try again?" Jo asked.

Mal shoved her hands into her pockets. "If I'm not the musical one, who am I!?"

And with that she moped into the cabin.

"Hey!" April appeared from around the cabin. "Who was in charge of moons?"

"MOONS? ME!" Ripley vaulted down from the roof. "Why?"

"Neptune has thirteen moons," April said, pointing at the walls of the cabin.

"AND I *made* thirteen moons," Ripley chirped. "I made them with paper and tape and glue and yellow sparkles and white sparkles and a few blue sparkles but not too many."

Ripley walked around the cabin, counting. "One, two, three, four, five, six, seven . . . eight, nine, ten, eleven, twelve . . . hey."

Molly shrugged. "You think they were counting moons?"

Jo was half listening, half looking at the trees and trying to drown out the voice of the letter that was still mumbling in the back of her brain, when she spotted, at the edge of the forest, a slip of white and a flash of yellow sparkle on what could very well be a runaway moon.

"There were thirteen here just a minute ago," Ripley frowned. "Swear to goddess!"

Suddenly Jo was off, running toward the woods, her flashlight bobbing in the dark.

"Hey!" April hollered. "Where the Roxane Gay are you going?"

CHAPTER 13

Sometimes the best way to find out where someone is going is to follow them. Quickly! Ripley was the first to catch up with Jo, with a Ripley-like burst of speed. "Where are we going?"

"I thought I saw something in the woods a few nights ago," Jo huffed, passing into the trees. "A mysterious glowing thing."

"What the junk!" April said, catching up. "You saw a mysterious glowing thing?" April pressed her lips together in an annoyed line. Which is hard to do when you're running.

"I didn't even know if it was a real thing!" Jo said, still running. "Also I can't tell you all the thoughts in my head all the time, April."

April threw her hands up. "What does that even mean? I tell you all mine!"

"Oh, look," Mal huffed, as she and Molly sprinted to catch up. "It's the running and talking part of our evening."

"At least this time there aren't any smelly unicorns," Molly noted.

"Yet," Mal added.

In the thick of the trees, under the light of the near-full moon, they assumed a reverse Lilith formation, which means standing in a circle with everyone facing out.

A convenient, circular way to cover ground.

"Okay," Jo said, shining her flashlight on the ground. "Everyone walk slow, look low."

"Got it," Ripley said. "What are we looking for?"

"A moon and a moon thief," Jo answered, searching the ground with her flashlight.

"OOO! OOO!" Ripley danced over a spot on the ground. "LOOK! THE GLITTER! THAT'S THE GLITTER I USED!"

Under the light of Ripley's flashlight, a thin trail of chunky holographic buttercup glittery specks twinkled. Ripley loved glitter so much, if she could safely eat glitter, she would.

"This," Jo said, kneeling down and touching her finger to a spot of glitter, "is what we're going to use to find the moon."

"Hansel and Glitter," April noted.

The glittery trail wound its way into the woods.

It wound its way into the deepest, darkest part of the woods, where the light of the camp could barely be seen. There, tucked behind some pines, was an ominous cave.

"We are standing outside a deep, dark cave." Molly whispered in a serious Dungeon Master-y voice. Molly, in addition to archery and raccoons, was a huge fan of board games and Dungeons and Dragons. Although her parents rarely let her play. "Do we enter?"

April shone her flashlight into the cave. The light barely cut into the blackness inside. "It's like a black hole," she said, her voice echoing in the darkness.

"Wait," Molly said, "is it possible this IS a black hole? Or a magical black hole? I ask because it seems within the realm of possibility."

Molly was right to be cautious; the difference between a magical black hole and a cave is one you rarely discover before it's too late.

Ripley stuck her head in. She cupped her hand next to her mouth. "Helloooooo."

Everyone listened.

Nothing.

"It sounds like a regular cave," Jo said.

"Well, no one's home," Mal cheered, turning to leave. "Guess it's time to go!"

Ripley tried again. "Hellllooooo. Is there anyone in there?"

Everyone listened.

There was a skittering sound.

"Great," Mal sighed. "Skittering. Skittering is the perfect sound for right now."

Jo stepped forward, flashlight pointed. "I'm going in."

Because there's no "Jo goes alone" in *team*, all the members of Roanoke advanced in slow, cautious steps, squinting in the dark.

The cave was cold, a void of light.

"What is that?" April's eyes grew wide.

"I think that's my heart beating," Molly said.

Jo felt something. A familiar tingle. "What was *that*?"

The sound of tiny, sharp breaths.

The scouts turned and aimed their flashlights at the sound in question. There, seemingly, stood Ripley's moon; glittery and glam with the flashlight beams hitting giant flecks of silver and sending tiny mirrors of white against the black of the cave. Something was holding up the moon, maybe like a shield.

"FREEZE!" April yelled out, although no one was moving. "DROP THE MOON AND PUT YOUR HANDS UP!"

"Okay, Cagney," Jo whispered, putting a gentle hand on April's back. "Easy does it."

April had been reading some more of the awesome Mermaid Lemonade Stand Mystery series, including the bestseller *Where Do You Think You're Going? FISHY!* Which is the one where the mermaid detective is always yelling, "PUT YOUR FINS UP!"

The moon was trembling.

"Heh heh, sorry about that," April said, her voice calmer and quieter. "Little overexcited."

"Hey," Jo added, in a soft and soothing voice. "We're not going to hurt you."

Slowly, the moon slid down, slightly, to reveal a tiny, furry, mousey face.

PART
TWO

HOSTING FOR THE BEST

"Be Our Guest"

Making your home, or the place where you are currently living, a space that is welcoming to newcomers is a vital skill. A Lumberjane is always ready to welcome a visitor to camp, to show them all the amazing things that being a scout has to offer, to share the joy that is being a Lumberjane.

Being a good host is as much about learning about your guest as it is about making sure your guest knows about all the things you know about the world. Every person we meet is an opportunity to learn something new, to expand our universe.

So the next time you're faced with a new face, a new encounter, don't forget to ...

CHAPTER 14

There are many available reactions a person, or creature, can have to seeing something unexpected. Ms. Annabella Panache, head of the drama club, overseer of the Be So Dramatic badge, teaches scouts the variety of classic reactions available to aspiring thespians.

Shock, with hands held up and next to the face, mouth and eyes open wide, is a good one.

Awe, with hands clapped over the mouth, is also nice.

If you do either of these poses with your body tipped backward, that's Shock and Awe. If you're frowning, that's Shock and Dismay.

While it was entirely surprising to the members of Roanoke to discover a well-dressed mouse in a cave with a moon, Shock and Awe were not their immediate responses.

I mean, yes, the fact that it was a MOUSE was sort of surprising.

But the members of Roanoke cabin once stood face to face with a Grootslang, which is a very large animal that looks a bit like a cross between an enormous alligator and a very angry elephant.

Sure, it's possible to be surprised after that.

But it takes a lot.

This mouse was about as tall as a loaf of bread if you stood it straight up and gave it a tail. Her fur was the color of lightly toasted toast, with the exception of her little ears and long tail, which were pink. She was wearing a shiny silk jacket that was the color of emeralds, which matched her eyes. She had big puffy sleeves and gold buttons, and looked very regal.

"I beg your pardon," she said, with a bit of what seemed like a British accent, her whiskers quivering as she clutched the foam moon with her tiny claws. "Is there something I can help you with?"

"We were just looking for our moon," Jo said, pointing, "which you seem to have."

"Oh yes." The mouse looked down at the moon clutched in her paws. "Quite right, quite right. Yes. I was just . . . taking it for a wee stroll."

"Oh," Ripley said. Because why wouldn't you take a moon for a walk?

Jo stepped forward. "Maybe we should introduce ourselves. I'm Jo." She pressed her hand against her chest then gestured at the curious campers behind her. "This is April, Mal, and Molly, and the person hugging you right now is Ripley."

Ripley wasn't so much hugging the mouse as she was bent over with her arms circled around this amazing mousey creature like a protective halo. It was taking just about every ounce of Ripley restraint for Ripley not to grab this clearly adorable creature and crush it into her chest in a massive hug.

"Hellooooo!" Ripley said, beaming down on the mouse with pure Ripley joy.

"It is a pleasure to meet you," the mouse said, bowing slightly.

Ripley, sensing the mouse needed space, stepped back, while continuing to beam at her.

"And you are?" Jo asked.

"Ah yes," the mouse smiled, possibly nervously. "Apologies. I am . . . Castor."

Castor looked up at the expectant faces lit by flashlights.

"From Saskatoon," Castor said.

"Saskatchewan," she added.

"52.1332° N, 106.6700° W?" she added again.

"Huh," Molly said.

"How specific," April noted. "And Canadian."

Jo threw a quick glance at April, who seamlessly caught it and threw a quick one back.

"Didn't mean to cause a bother," Castor said, holding out the moon.

"Okay," Jo said, reaching forward and taking the moon from Castor's outstretched paw. "Well. Now that we've got our moon, we're going to head back to our cabin. Because it's late."

Jo considered. The cave was ice cold and damp, and it did not look like an ideal place to leave anyone, let alone something as sweet and fuzzy looking as Castor. So she said, "You're welcome to join us."

"Oh my." Castor looked around. "I wouldn't want to put you at any inconvenience."

"No inconven—" April began.

"IT WILL BE AWESOME!" Ripley gushed, with the best of intentions and a bucket of Ripley exuberance. "You can even sleep on my bunk, because I technically have two bunks so there's TONS of room!"

"Well, I suppose, if it's absolutely no trouble," Castor said, "then, that would be very lovely."

"YAY!" Ripley sprang forward and swung Castor up on her shoulders. "LET'S GO!"

"Rip," Jo cautioned, "you have to ask before you swing someone up on your shoulders."

"Ha ha," Castor chuckled, grabbing onto Ripley's shoulder to steady herself. "It's quite all right. Thank you, Ripley."

And with that, Ripley was off skipping back to camp with Castor bouncing on her shoulders, her heart bursting with happiness.

April stood next to Jo, who stood next to Mal, who stood next to Molly.

"Recap," April said. "Talking mouse. Fancy coat. Moon thief."

"Possibly moon borrower," Jo noted.

"From 'Saskatchewan,'" April said, using air quotes, which a person generally uses when they don't fully believe something.

"British accent," Molly added.

"Canadian accent?" Mal wondered.

It was, admittedly, an odd combination.

But.

"Not the oddest combination we've come across," Molly said.

"So we're keeping our Lumberjane senses on alert," April noted.

"Yes, we are," Jo said. "We'll also go check in with Rosie in the morning."

Thinking about Rosie made her think about the letter she still had folded in her pocket. A letter that was, for Jo, figuratively but not actually, even bigger than a talking mouse.

"Won't Jen, like, immediately notice that we have a talking mouse in our cabin?" Molly added, as they headed back to the cabin.

Jen might have noticed if she was not up to her eyebrows dealing with stuff for Galaxy Wars. She'd left a note for the cabin on her pillow, which read, simply, GO TO SLEEP.

So they did.

Hey. A talking mouse doesn't mean you don't still have to get a good night's sleep.

Within minutes of heads hitting pillows, most of Roanoke, including their newest guest, was sound asleep.

Except for Jo, who lay in bed, thinking.

CHAPTER 15

Recipients of the Lumberjane Time After Time badge know that people who were around a long time ago used the sun and moon to tell time.

The earth going around the sun once = a year.

A full orbit of the moon = a month.

Eventually, to make thing easier and more exact, some scientific types came up with (ta da!) the second.

A second is an actual thing that exists outside whatever it is you use to tell time (cuckoo clock, cell phone, old-timey pocket watch). Which you can find out more about by looking up the number: 9192631770.

Sixty seconds is a minute. Sixty minutes is an hour. Twenty-four hours is a day. Three hundred and sixty-five days makes a year.

A decade is how long a night feels when you're nervous about something and don't know what to do.

Jo had spent her night silently arguing with the letter, still shoved in her pocket, about alternate realities.

Specifically, the letter had made its case for the undeniable benefits of the program it was now calling S.T.A.A.R.

Think of it this way, the letter said, its voice sure, being a scientist is your destiny, correct?

Correct, Jo thought. I mean, I think so.

That's a yes?

Yes.

So then what's the problem? The letter seemed on the edge of exasperated.

By the time the sun rose, the voice in Jo's head was hoarse. And Jo still didn't know what to do, although she was pretty sure lying awake in bed, arguing with a voice no one else could hear, wasn't helping.

This is what scientists DO, the letter insisted. They don't sit around at summer camp getting baking badges and canoeing. They move on and spend their summers in rooms lit with energy-saving bulbs and get down to the matter of improving the world as we know it with knowledge!

But, Jo thought. *I don't want to leave.*

Well, the letter began, only to be interrupted by—

"RISE AND SHINE!" April's eyes peeked over the edge of the bunk. "What are you doing? Let me guess."

"Thinking," Jo said quietly, because that seemed to be the most accessible description for what was going on in her head.

April scrunched her eyebrows up in a concerned BFF look that said, but did not say out loud, "I am worried about whatever it is you're thinking about."

Jo felt her best friend's worried gaze like a small weight in her hand.

This is the thing about having a friend with whom you have developed a psychic bond. There's a part of you that's always connected to them and vice versa, like a string you cannot break.

It is the greatest and most complicated phenomenon known to scouts, this bond. This string that is endlessly stretchable and able to tie you in knots.

Which is not to say April knew what to do over on her side of the string, except send Jo an endless stream of psychic emails saying, "I'm here. No matter what."

"Ready for breakfast?" Jo asked.

Which was weird because when was the last time Jo even ate breakfast?

"I'm ready when you are," April said.

"Hey," Mal sat up in bed. "Have either of you seen our fuzzy guest and our blue-haired cabin mate?"

It was early enough that the camp still had that "just woke up" vibe, the sun just starting to turn the sky blue from purple.

Few enough people were up that no one had spotted Castor. Not when she crept out of Roanoke cabin, not when she scurried across the grass to the kitchen, not even as she sat crouched next to the back door of the mess hall, sniffing at the air with her little pink nose, her eyes darting this way and that as she slowly, but surely, crept forward.

No one except . . .

"WHO goes there?" BunBun hollered from behind the screen door. She was dressed in a tinfoil cap and tiger ears and was carrying a drum made out of a can of beans.

"I beg your pardon!" Castor tumbled backward.

"Hey, BunBun! It's me and my new friend, Castor," Ripley chirped, appearing from around the corner.

"Oh," said Castor. "Uh. Yes. Hello."

BunBun turned and marched back into the mess hall. "I'M VERY BUSY."

"Your guards are very robust in their duties," Castor said, nervously rubbing her paws together.

"Ha ha, BunBun's not a guard!" Ripley pressed her face against the screen. "She's just awesome."

Castor looked like she wanted to run. Her tail twitched.

"Are you hungry?" Ripley asked.

"Oh." Castor twitched her tail again. "Um, not terribly. Just perhaps a mite peckish."

Ripley grinned. "You like cheese, right? Cuz we have lots of cheese. I like Beemster and Burrata and American Cheddar but there's regular Canadian Cheddar too if you like."

"Oh," Castor said lightly, running a paw over her ear in a casual mousey gesture. "Is there?"

Pushing open the door, Ripley peered inside. "Yeah! Technically we're supposed to wait for breakfast but sometimes Kzzyzy lets me grab a snack. HEY, KZZYZY!"

"WHAT?!"

Kzzyzy was in an acrobatic flurry of pots and pans, and she barely looked up to see that Ripley had a guest.

"I'm just getting a snack," Ripley called out.

"Don't mess up my larder!" Kzzyzy called back over the howling of Mama Cass.

"I'M VERY BUSY!" BunBun shouted from somewhere in the kitchen.

Ripley and Castor wound their way past many mixing bowls and a series of burners, all of which had things furiously bubbling on the top.

"Here is where they keep the bird seed," Ripley said, as they walked past a room full of barrels.

"Here is where Rosie keeps all her special stuff," Ripley said, pointing at a door that seemed to have a bit of a green glow coming out from underneath.

"Here's where we keep all the stuff I think *you'll* like," Ripley said, pushing open a metal door.

Inside were shelves and shelves and shelves of cheese.

So much cheese that the air seemed to be heavy with mozzarella.

Castor's whiskers quivered. "This is q-quite a supply," she stammered.

Ripley took a tiny chunk of cheddar from one of the wheels and handed it to Castor. "Here you go!"

"Thank you," Castor said, as she curled her claw around the slice, her eyes still roaming here and there, taking in the cheese, the door, and the missing padlock that was no longer on the door, because BunBun was using it as a necklace.

Not that anyone had noticed.

Except for Castor.

"We should get going," Ripley said, stepping out. "Breakfast is soon. There will be tons more food there."

"Tons. Quite," Castor whispered, running her claw along the shelf, careful to pick up her tail as Ripley shut the door. "Indeed."

89

CHAPTER 16

After breakfast, with Jen busy with Galaxy Wars stuff and nowhere to be found, Roanoke marched over to Rosie's cabin to ask if Rosie thought it would be okay if Castor stayed in the cabin.

"How long do you plan on staying?" Rosie inquired.

"Oh, a day or two at most." Castor assured her. "Just passing through."

"Aw," Ripley grumbled, hanging her head. "Don't leave yet."

"I think a few days is okay. We'll just need some sort of notice from a parent or guardian to let us know someone knows you're here," Rosie said, rubbing her chin.

"Oh, quite right," Castor nodded. "I could get in touch

with someone, yes, of course. My whereabouts on this plan—er, in this place, are certainly known."

"Excellent," Rosie boomed, as she coiled a very long silver chain on a rather large spool sitting on her desk. "So a letter of some sort shouldn't be a problem."

Castor shook her head. "Certainly not."

"Well, that was shockingly easy," Molly said, as they left the cabin. "What do you want to do now?"

"Um . . ." Mal was already stepping away. "I have to go practice my song," she said.

April had her Surf's Up badge, which meant spending her day with Seafarin' Karen.

"Hang ten, dudes!" she called, as she ran to get changed into her board shorts.

Ripley had to work on her Sew Be It badge, although she was sorry to go. "I'll be back real fast," she promised Castor, and she bounced off.

Castor adjusted the cuffs on her jacket. "Well then," she said, looking in the direction of the mess hall and the unguarded cheese, "I suppose I will just acquaint myself with the local grounds while you all are off doing your relative duties."

"Hey! We could give you a tour!" Molly piped in.

Technically, Molly's varied experiences with tours of various historic monuments had been that they were pretty dry experiences with plaques and posing next to plaques, but camp was way more interesting than the site of the factory that made the first safety pins, Molly's father's favorite.

"That's a great idea," Jo said. Because Jo was looking for a distraction from the piece of paper in her pocket, and because Jo wanted to keep an eye on Castor.

"Oh, I don't want to be a bother," Castor protested. "I'm sure you have better and more important things to do than to escort me about."

"Actually," Jo said, "showing you around is kind of a Lumberjane thing."

"A Lumberjane . . . thing?" Castor tilted her head.

"Helping," Jo explained, "is kind of a Lumberjane thing. Like something we try to do as Lumberjanes. Anyway, I'm sure there's lots of stuff around here that would be of interest to you. What are some of your hobbies?"

"Oh," Castor scratched her head. "Hobbies? I'm sorry, not familiar with the term."

"You know," Molly said, adjusting the slumbering raccoon on her head. "Like the things you like to do, like pottery or, um, painting or whatever?"

Castor squinted. "Sorry. Still not following."

"Okay, well," Jo started walking across the grass. "We'll just start walking around and pointing at things and telling you things and you can shout out any questions."

Castor gave a tiny mouse shrug and followed Molly and Jo toward the center of camp.

Just about every square inch of the camp was covered in scouts doing what scouts do, including: team jump rope (for the Skip It badge), weaving, boxing, and a round of tai chi.

"So this is a pretty typical day at camp," Molly said. "Which means it's pretty kernuts around here."

Castor wasn't sure what a kernut was but assumed it was a type of cheese.

Castor squinted and pointed. "What's that?"

"That's Jazzercise," Molly said, holding her hands up and waving her fingers in demonstration. "Which is not really a word. But it's like a dance-y exercise, I guess? I believe that move is technically a RuPaul shimmy."

"Blimey." Castor's nose twitched. "And why would you spend your time doing something like that?"

"It's good exercise," Jo offered. "Good for flexibility and coordination."

"And it's FUN," Molly said.

Castor hopped over to Jo's other shoulder and pointed to a figure running through the camp with great speed. "And is that also Jazzysize?"

Jo squinted. "Um. Oh. Actually, I think that's someone getting chased by a bee."

"Goodness." Castor shook her head. Sniffed the air. Pointed. "And are those also for Jazzysize?"

Molly stepped over to where Castor was pointing and picked up a white volleyball, tossing it in the air. "These are volleyball courts."

"And what do you use the net for?"

"You hit the ball over it," Jo explained.

"Then what?" Castor ran a paw over her whiskers.

"Well. Then someone hits it back." Molly said.

"And why do you do that?" Castor wondered.

"It's a great cardiovascular workout," Jo began. "Hand-eye coordination . . ."

"And it's FUN," Molly added emphatically.

"This is a very strange place," Castor said quietly. "A strange, FUN planet."

The last leg of the tour was the arts and crafts cabin.

"And this," Molly explained, throwing open the doors, "is where we make things!"

Jo put her hand down on one of the tables next to a pile of felt.

Castor crept down her arm, her body twitching. "What . . ." she stammered. "This is . . ."

Castor cautiously crawled up to a bucket of buttons of all shapes and sizes and plunged her paw inside to pull out a large green button the size of her face.

"All of this," she said, her voice hushed. "You can just… take?"

"Yeah, there's pipe cleaners and anything long and bendy on this wall, this wall is for round and shiny, this wall is for paint, and this wall," Molly said, gesturing, "is Ripley's favorite, THE GLITTER WALL."

Castor stepped forward and pushed her paw into a bucket of yellow sparkles. "Glitter," she said, her voice hushed.

"We could make a moon now if you want," Jo said.

Castor looked up. Stunned. "You want to *make* a moon?"

"We can make whatever you want," Jo said, looking around. "I think we just need some Styrofoam."

"Why would we MAKE a moon?" Castor asked, sinking her paw back into the glitter.

"Well," Jo tilted her head. "You could make a moon using precise existing measurements and that could—"

"Because it's FUN," Molly said, pulling out a pair of scissors. "Also, it's super easy. I'll show you."

"Right," Jo added, grabbing a tube of glue. "Fun."

"This fun thing," Castor marveled, "is quite the stuff down here."

95

CHAPTER 17

By the end of the day, Castor was covered in glitter. It clung to her coat and her tail. It shook out of her fur every time she stepped or breathed or blinked or thought about something. And it appeared to make her very happy.

She lay flat on her back on the picnic table, next to her moon mobile, shivering with glee.

"FUN," she sighed. "That was FUN?"

"Yes." Molly smiled, turning her face into the sun and listening to Bubbles snooze.

Jo nodded.

Thinking about how great it was to be a Lumberjane, Jo felt like her insides were a centrifuge, which is like this

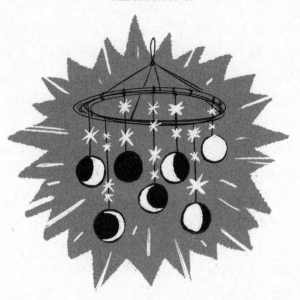

rapidly spinning thing that scientists use to separate matter. And the centrifuge was just spinning and spinning inside her, even though on the outside she looked like Jo, who had taken a talking mouse on a tour of the most important place in the world.

Sure, FUN. And then, the letter said, eventually you move on to more important things. Yes?

"It's just FUN here, all the time?" Castor asked, looking at the glitter on her fur.

"Not all the time," Molly noted. "But there's definitely a lot of fun around. We still do, like, learn things. Like we all earn badges . . ."

"Badges," Castor said. "Fine cloth?"

"More like markers of achievement," Molly explained, pulling her That's Accordion to You badge out of her pocket to show Castor.

Castor sniffed it. "Very nice," she offered, politely.

Off in the distance, Molly spotted Mal sitting on a picnic bench, her fingers working the keys of her accordion.

Jo looked at Castor. "So how is it you ended up here, again?"

Castor's furry cheeks seemed to blush a bit.

"Oh, I just looked down and there you were," Castor said, running her paw over her nose. "And this place has a lovely reputation for . . ."

"Looked down from where?" Jo asked.

"Lovely reputation for what?" Molly asked.

"What? OH!" Castor shook her furry head. "I—"

Just then Ripley, much to Castor's relief, bounded over with a particularly Ripley-like bounce.

"SPECIAL DELIVERY!" she hollered.

Holding her hands behind her back, Ripley stopped in front of Castor. "Ready?"

Castor curled back on her hind legs. "Oh. Yes, I suppose so."

"TADA!" Ripley whipped out a slightly rough-edged but still very cool tiny jean vest, just Castor's size, covered in little patches in a rainbow of colors.

Castor blinked her green eyes, the breath suddenly pushed out of her little mouse body.

"It's for YOU!" Ripley said, holding it up. "I hope it fits. It's my first vest."

Castor reached forward, taking the vest from Ripley. "You made this?" She touched it to her chest. "For me?"

"SURE!"

Ripley did a little dance as Castor slipped off her tiny green jacket and slipped on her present. It was a little big, but still pretty cool.

"Vest vest vest vest vest VEST!" Ripley sang. "Vest vest vest vest vest VEST!"

"Great moonstones and rings of fire," Castor breathed, looking down at it, "'Tis by far the most glorious garment I have ever seen in any galaxy."

Jo raised an eyebrow. "'Tis it?"

Ripley blushed, pulling a few stray bits of thread out of her hair. "Aw shucks. I just wanted you to feel, you know, like part of the cabin and everything."

"That's super nice, Rip," Molly said, patting Ripley on the back.

"Castor, your coat, it's . . . intricate," Jo said, running her fingers over the gold embroidery on Castor's coat, a lustrous fabric unlike any she had ever seen, in this galaxy or any other. The bottom was covered in little gold stars. It weighed no more than half a penny.

Castor was too busy running her claw along the slightly crooked stitches of the vest to hear. "For me," she whispered. "Astonishing."

"Wouldn't it be cool if you could stay here forever," Ripley said. "Just like us?"

"Quite," Castor said, her voice small.

Jo's stomach flipped.

Everyone has to go sometime, the letter said, in a voice no one else could hear that rang in Jo's ears.

CHAPTER 18

That night, dinner was Kzzyzy's specialty: six-cheese lasagna. Bubbles watched, unamused, from his perch on Molly's head, as Castor devoured a slice twice her size.

Bubbles was somehow not Castor's biggest fan.

That night, the whole mess hall seemed to be under a spell—it was so quiet you could hear the Parmesan shakers shaking.

"What's going on?" Ripley whispered, eyes wide. "It's so quiet I can hear my teeth."

"Maybe everyone's nervous for Galaxy Wars," Molly suggested.

April looked at Jo, thinking this was probably not why

Jo, who was quiet anyway, was sitting so still, with her eyes fixed on something close and far away.

"Pardon me," Castor said, wiping a piece of cheese off her whisker, "but this Galaxy event in which you are engaged, it is a battle?"

"It's more of a contest," Molly offered.

"But you must challenge your fellow cabins, and to the victor go the spoils," Castor said. "Correct?"

As if woken from a spell, April raised her head.

"You bet your deep-fried vegan cheesesticks," she said. "If we win this, we'll always be the first cabin to win Galaxy Wars. AND we'll get our portrait in the hall of winning stuff. AND . . ." April paused, putting her fork to her lips. "That's it, actually."

"The pin thingy!" Ripley chimed in.

"RIGHT!" April said. "THE PIN THINGY!"

"Quite . . . curious that you're . . . excited to receive a portrait," Castor whispered, incredulous. "When you have so much cheese!"

Jo looked up. She'd forgotten about the portrait. "That would be pretty cool."

Technically Roanoke cabin was a pretty accomplished group of scouts, masters of adventure and discovery. But still. Winning as a team was something they hadn't done.

Jo knew well the light flashing in April's eyes, tiny electric fires that signaled a burst of determination.

Jo couldn't imagine being a Lumberjane without April. And it was highly probable that the same was true for April.

There was actually almost nothing Jo wouldn't do for April, with the exception of reading Mermaid Lemonade Stand books, which Jo found relatively predictable in terms of plot.

"What's the score?" Jo asked. "Of the competition?"

"We tied for second in cabin decoration," April said, ticking the points off on her fingers. "So we're tied with Zodiac."

That would be a pretty nice way to leave, the letter noted, weighing in on, seemingly, everything now, from Jo's pocket. Maybe take the sting out a bit for the people you'll leave behind.

April raised an eyebrow. It wasn't like Jo to think about stuff like points, even though Jo thought about a good many things. Worrying about stuff like points was an April thing.

Worrying about the basic mechanics of the world around her was a Jo thing.

Mal worried about water and the number of things they were forced to do on a daily basis that had to do with water.

Jo looked down at her lasagna.

I could win Galaxy Wars, she thought. *That would make April happy.*

Just then there was a familiar CLANG! CLANG! CLANG!

"SCOUTS! THE NEXT ROUND OF GALAXY WARS IS IN FIVE MINUTES! PLEASE HEAD TO THE NORTHEAST PADDOCK!"

Jo stood up. "Let's go win this *thing,*" she said.

It was not a very Jo thing to say, April thought.

Not a very Jo thing at all.

CHAPTER 19

It was difficult to guess in advance what the next event in Galaxy Wars would be. TRIVIA sure, okay, but what kind of TRIVIA?

Being a Lumberjane means a lot of things are something obvious PLUS something else.

"It could be trivia plus a giant pillow fight," Ripley suggested, as they took their place behind their cabin flag.

"I beg your pardon," Castor's whiskers twitched. "You lot fight with *pillows*?"

"It's kind of weird, but sometimes, yes," Molly said.

"And this is FUN as well?" Castor asked.

"Oh my gosh, yes," Ripley bounced. "YES YES YES."

"Why do you think it's a pillow fight, Rip?" Jo asked.

"Because that's where my head usually is when the moon is out," Ripley explained.

Castor shook her head. "The moon is always out, you just can't see it from where you are."

"WELCOME TO THE NEXT EVENT OF GAL-AXY WARS!" Jen shouted.

Jen looked tired. Her hair was poofed out like a cloud around her head, and her beret was askew.

"Today you will be competing in a first-ever Lumber-jane event, HAMSTER BALL TRIVIA CROQUET!"

"Whaaaaat?!" April's mouth dropped open as a herd of camp counselors rolled a bunch of giant clear plastic, rubber balls onto the field.

"HAMSTER BALL!" Zodiac crowed together.

"I think Zodiac really likes Hamster Balls," Molly said, watching as Zodiac did a little dance to celebrate . . . hamster balls.

"OKAY!" Jen wobbled slightly, her body elastic with exhaustion. "I'm going to pass you over to VANESSA to explain this event!"

Vanessa grabbed the megaphone. "OKAY, SCOUTS, LISTEN UP! Each cabin is going to choose a BALL scout and a MALLET scout! The BALL scout's job will be to roll their BALL in the right direction. The MALLET scout's job is give the ball ONE GIANT push or kick or whatever works for you."

"It's all about the ball," Jo murmured as she stared at the field, deciphering the best method for getting the ball from one end of the field to the other.

"At each corner of the field," Vanessa continued, "the counselors will be holding up a card with potential ANSWERS to each question. The team who gets the most answers correct wins twenty-five points!"

A huddle was in order.

"I got this," Jo said, poking her chest.

April looked at Jo. "Yeah?"

"Yeah."

"Maybe we should do it together," April offered.

"I like this plan," Molly said, feeling neither here nor there about being in a giant hamster ball.

Ripley gave a thumbs-up. "You guys are awesome!"

April held out her left hand for a patented April and Jo handshake.

Which goes a little like this.

THE 4(ish) ELEMENTS of Jo & April's Super Secret BFF HANDSHAKE

1 WAVE CHOP! (WATER)

Bend arm at a 90° angle and touch elbows

Pro Level: Keep eye contact the whole time

EXPERT: KEEP EYES Closed!

2 WIND GUST (AIR)

Flip up forearms and link thumbs

Clap Back of Hands

2.A

2.B Move

2.C to

LINK THUMBS

3 FLICKERY FLAME (FIRE)

4 PEACE on (EARTH)

Keeping thumbs linked bring hands up, wiggling fingers (it kinda looks like a fire consuming oxygen to grow taller? Right? Totally.)

Bring hands down to form bunny ears (or substitute a hand sign for another noble creature of Earth).

ex.

Wolf   Llama   Goose   Hairy Tarantula

And with that, Jo speed-walked onto the field.

"I think I know how to make the ball move at maximum velocity!" Jo shouted.

"Okay, well, how about dialing it back!" April huffed. "Until we get on the field!"

By the time April caught up to Jo in the center of the massive croquet arena, Jo was already shutting the door on the giant hamster ball, locking herself inside.

Jo tapped on the plastic. "Kick up!" she shouted. "I'll do the rest."

"Hey! There's no 'I'll do the rest' in team," April said, tapping back on the plastic. She also wanted to shout, "WHAT THE MAE JEMISON IS GOING ON WITH YOU?"

But there was no time.

"On your MARIA!" Vanessa hollered. "GET SEEMA!"

"GERTRUDE!"

"First question!" Jen shouted into the megaphone. "I am a very small solar system body made mostly of ices mixed with smaller amounts of dust and rock and I am hurtling . . ."

"It's a COMET!" April screamed, turning the giant ball in the right direction. "COMET! COMET! COMET!"

109

"I GOT IT!" Jo spotted the counselor holding up the sign that read COMET. "GO!"

April gave the hamster ball a whopping April-size roundhouse KICK and Jo, holding her hands out to keep herself steady, began running as fast as she could, looking not unlike a frantic giant hamster, neck and neck with Wren from Zodiac, heading to the west corner of the field.

"I'm just going to say it," Molly said, watching Jo human ping-pong from corner to corner, "I'm really glad I'm not in a hamster ball right now."

Mal nodded.

"Why is it called a hamster ball?" Castor asked, sitting on Ripley's shoulder.

"We put hamsters in balls like that sometimes," Molly said.

"I BEG YOUR PARDON, YOU DO WHAT?"

Several questions later, the score was tied: three questions right for both Zodiac and Roanoke, with Dartmoor and Woolpit in a close second with two correct each.

Ripley gripped her hands together. "Last question," she whispered.

A hush fell over the field.

Zodiac crossed their fingers and toes.

On the field, the tension was so thick you could cut it with a cheese knife.

Hes stepped back and prepared to BOOT. "We got this, girl!"

"We're tied," Jo fumed, fogging up her hamster ball as she paced. "The only way to win is to get there first!"

"FINAL ANSWER," Vanessa hollered, holding up a giant card, "Is the name of THIS CONSTELLATION!

AAAAAAAND GO!!!!"

April squinted, her brain gears furiously whirring. "What the junk is it?"

"I don't know." Jo could feel sweat beading on the back of her neck.

Zodiac was already rolling, bounding across the grass.

Jo blinked. "It's Cygnus!"

April spun around, trying to get a better look at the other answers. "Are you—"

"It's Cygnus, the Swan!" Jo shouted. "Give me a kick!"

"Okay." April took several steps back, winding up. "One APRIL SPECIAL comin' up!"

And with that, April gave the biggest boot anyone has ever give a hamster ball in the history of time.

"Oh goodness." Castor hopped up onto the top of Mal's head, clutching her paws together. "Where is she going?"

Ripley covered her mouth. "What's wrong?"

April's massive boot sent Jo hurtling across the field.

"She's going in the wrong ruddy direction," Castor said, just as Zodiac rolled into the correct answer, Cassiopeia, to win.

CHAPTER 20

The Lumberjanes have a rich history of magnificent, and sometimes strange, inventions. One of the most prolific Lumberjane inventors, prior to Jo, was Mary Margaret Wollstonecraft Pomodore III, who invented one of the first time machines.

Before disappearing into a puff of purple smoke one night, while holding what many claimed was a light bulb in one hand and a box of chocolate cherries in the other, Mary Margaret had often argued that time was mostly an annoying thing that a person should be able to alter.

Mary Margaret was very fond of "redos," in basketball, golf, and life, and many wondered what wrong it was she had disappeared into history to right.

Probably we will never know.

Listening as Zodiac cabin celebrated their victory with several rounds of the Pointer Sisters' "I'm So Excited" on the accordion, Jo knew EXACTLY what she wished SHE could go back and redo if she had a light bulb and Mary Margaret's secret notebook (which was actually hidden . . . not that far from where Jo was sitting).

April sat down, carefully, next to Jo. "So. I think I know the answer to this, but, if I asked you what was going on would you have no comet?"

"No comet," Jo said, looking up at the sky full of constellations she did know, like the Big and Little Dipper.

"Generally speaking, you're not usually the 'I have to win' person in the group," April observed, while also observing Jo's face. "That's kind of my claim to fame."

"I just thought it would be a nice thing," Jo said, still looking at the sky. "To win."

"Sure. But. There will be other quests," April said, patting Jo on the back. "Other victories. Right?"

"Sure," Jo said, although it was hard to say that and look April in the eye, so she looked at the moon instead, which was looking back down at Jo like the giant all-knowing eye the moon can be on a clear summer night.

It was the smallest "sure" Jo had ever uttered, about the size of a sliver of cheese left on a plate, too small for a piece of toast or even a cracker.

Under the same moon, Castor and Ripley sat in the courtyard, munching from a snack plate that was almost out of cheddar and crackers.

"So, you know a lot about stars, huh?" Ripley said, brushing crumbs off her shirt.

"Oh, yes I suppose so," Castor said, adjusting her vest. "I spend quite a bit of time with them . . . at home."

"I spend a lot of time with my brothers and my sisters and my mom and my dad and our cat," Ripley said. "At home."

"Do you miss them?" Castor said, looking up at the stars.

"Sometimes," Ripley said, taking the second-last bit of cheese. "But mostly I love being at camp because camp is the best."

Castor took a nibble of her cheese, clutched in her little claws. She was still amazed how it was just being handed out willy-nilly. "What's your favorite part? Is it Jazzysize?"

Ripley wobbled her head. "I don't even have a favorite part. Because every day is a favorite part? Like sometimes my favorite part is a waterfall. Sometimes it's a T. Rex. Sometimes it's climbing a tree. Sometimes it's swimming with April and Jo and Molly. Sometimes it's dancing with Bubbles. Sometimes it's discovering something new. Sometimes it's doing something I love doing again . . ."

"That sounds," Castor looked at the last piece of cheese on the plate, "fun."

"Yeah," Ripley sighed. "Normally, we're way more fun than we were today. I mean, you know, today was fun. But it's usually way way funner."

Castor nodded. "I myself have always preferred discovery to pillaging. Although sometimes pillaging is necessary, obviously, for survival. But I think discovery is much closer to what you call . . . fun."

Ripley nodded, wondering if pillaging meant what she thought it meant.

Castor pushed the plate with the last piece of cheese toward Ripley. "You know, once, several moons ago, my mother and I found this place. You would love it." She smiled, rubbing her paws together. "It was made of little stones, all shaped like tiny buttons, all white and black, and when you ran over them, the ground made a noise like tacka-de-tacka-de-tacka-de-tacka! I loved that sound. I would have gone back many times just to hear it. Such a ridiculous sound."

"That sounds really cool," Ripley said. "Tacka-de-tacka-de-tacka-de-tacka!"

"You all are so lovely and kind," Castor said, looking down at the plate, thinking about cheese, about the larder she had planned to raid that very night. "I hadn't expected that. I hadn't expected any of this."

Ripley lay down on top of the picnic bench. Castor did the same.

"The moon always makes me think of a face looking down," Ripley said, closing one eye.

"Ripley?"

"Yes?"

Castor shifted her ears. "I have to tell you something."

117

CHAPTER 21

By the time everyone got to bed—with the exception of Jen, who was, surprise surprise, out working on Galaxy Wars stuff—it was pretty late.

Ripley and Castor passed out on their bunk, fully clothed and full of cheese.

Crickets chirped outside.

The cabin was quiet.

April was thinking.

Crawling up to Jo's bunk, she asked, "Remember the games we used to play, you know, pre–Galaxy Wars?"

Jo considered. "Like, What Time Is It Mrs. Wolf?"

"Gah, the abomination that is What Time Is It Mrs. Wolf!" April shook her fist at the ceiling. "SLOWEST RACE EVER."

"Yeah."

Molly rolled over on her bunk. "Did you guys ever play Simon Says?"

"We played SIMONE Says," Jo said. "Because April refused to do what Simon said."

"I'm rarely in a mood to be dictated to by a fictional male figure," April sniffed.

"Who is?" Mal wondered.

"What was that other game," April mused, "that one you used to think was so funny . . . ?"

Jo lay back on her pillow. "Funny?"

"The one about the moon," April mused, looking up at the bottom of Jo's bunk.

"OH!" Jo grinned. "HA HA!"

It was the first time in so many days April had heard Jo laugh, and it filled her heart.

"Man," Jo chuckled, "I loved that game, what was it called?"

There was a crashing sound outside, and Jen stumbled in the door.

"Hey, guys," she slurred sleepily. "It's Joan. Or Jen. Whatever. Go to sleep."

She swiveled and stumbled back out again.

"Is it me," Molly said, mostly to herself, "or are things, like, super stressful at camp right now?"

Mal had fallen asleep, still strapped to her accordion.

"Good night, everyone," Jo said, reaching to turn off the light.

On any given night, a person has any number of dreams, which we often forget because waking up tends to jog them out of our heads.

Jo dreamed she was standing in front of two doors. In front of one was the letter, with cartoon legs and arms and a deep, serious voice.

Hey, Jo.

In front of the other was April, who was yelling and waving her arms and saying something Jo couldn't hear.

Mal dreamed she was standing on a giant pizza, in her underwear, playing the accordion, except all the buttons were in the wrong places and the keys didn't make any sounds.

Finally, Mal slammed her fingers down and there was a KABOOM!

Mal sat up, awake. "PIZZA!?"

BOOM! CRASH!

The door slammed open and a green light filled the cabin.

And was gone as fast as it had come.

Molly sat up. "WHAT THE JUNK WAS THAT!?"

"IS EVERYONE OKAY?" Jo called out.

"I think so." April rubbed her eyes.

Everyone looked around.

A cold wind blew through the open door, tossing the twinkly moons over Ripley's bed.

Ripley jumped up on her bed. "CASTOR!"

"WHAT?" everyone yelled in unison.

"SHE'S GONE!"

CHAPTER 22

A Lumberjane, amongst many other things, is always prepared. There are many ways to achieve this. One is knowing a lot about a lot of different things so you can be prepared to answer questions like: "What is the best way to treat a sunburn?" or "How do you make a slingshot?" or "How many games does it take to beat a Mammoth Marsupial Mouthmonster at chess?"

(Aloe.)

(Find a natural Y-shaped branch, trim, add notches to the top forks one inch below the tips, attach flexible tubing with a leather pouch in the center at the notches. Fire away.)

(Actually, this is a bit of a trick question, since Mammoth Marsupials don't play chess, they play checkers. Very well.)

The other is to have some basic supplies with you at all

times so that you are prepared for the series of unexpected events that are an inevitable part of being a Lumberjane, most especially when you are a member of Roanoke cabin.

This is why April, when she sprung out of her bunk, already had her lasso in hand.

"ROANOKE TO THE LASSO!"

Ripley, who was prepared with cat-like reflexes, was out of the cabin like a cannonball in two-point-two seconds FLAT. She shot out the door and bounced twice on the ground, landing in classic superhero pose in the clearing just beyond the cabins.

"CASTOR?"

A sharp squeak pierced the air.

Ripley clutched her fist. "Castor!"

She bounced and bounced across the courtyard until she spotted what at first looked like a massive black cloud with many legs, and which was, in fact, rumbling toward her at that very moment, with Castor bumping around on the top.

"Rrrrripley!"

Ripley bounded, jumped, and landed on the top of the moving mass, right next to a very rattled-looking Castor!

"Are you okay?" Ripley asked, huffing.

The moving black mass with many legs wriggled and skittered over the ground.

"I believe so," Castor grumbled. "No thanks to you ruddy CHEESE HEADS!" she shouted down at the rumbling mass beneath them.

Ripley looked down. Ripley had ridden a moose and a giant kitten. This was new, though. "Uh," she said, her voice bouncing along with the rumbling creatures below them. "Soooo, what's happening?"

April, Jo, Mal, and Molly ran out the door and spotted the mass carrying Castor and Ripley in the distance. It seemed to be headed toward the camp entrance.

"We can catch them if we cut through . . ." Mal paused. "Uh."

"The cabins!" Molly shouted, as she dodged past Dartmoor and rounded the corner past Zodiac's cabin.

"Then what do we do?" Mal shouted as they ran.

"Sling shots?" Molly called back.

"We don't know what that thing carrying them is," Jo huffed. "Or what will happen if we hit whatever it is."

Scientists like to consider the many outcomes of what they might do before they do it.

Lumberjanes know that the first rule of firing a slingshot is you want to know what you're firing at and why you're firing.

"WHATEVER IT IS, BRING IT ON," April hollered, whipping her lasso in the air.

"You know," Mal huffed, "as a side note, I never run and talk when I'm at home."

They made it to the camp entrance ahead of the mass, but it was closing in.

"Right." April looked up at the arch above the entrance. "Here's the plan: two times two scout Missy Deville Dodow move followed by a basic Limbo rescue."

"You want to add a half Andie Walsh into that?" Molly asked.

April scrunched up her eyebrows. "What's that?"

Molly grinned. "I don't actually think that's a move. I just think it should be."

"Right!" April raised her hand. "We have the will and the way! Roanoke ready?"

"Check!"

"Check!"

"Check!"

Ripley looked down. Looking closer, the moving mass was a mass of creatures, all wearing silver goggles and tiny silver helmets, with massive clawed hands, which were currently all lifted up to carry their passengers. Little pink noses snuffed the air. Purely out of curiosity, Ripley asked, "What are we being carried away by?"

"Moon moles." Castor frowned. "RUDDY AWFUL MOON MOLES!"

The mass of moon moles took a twist to the left and to the right before doubling back in their original direction.

"Do they know where they're going?" Ripley asked, looking behind her.

"Probably not," Castor said. "They've got brie for brains, these things."

That's not exactly true, but Castor was feeling pretty annoyed at that moment.

"Okay, cool." Ripley looked up and spotted her cabin mates getting into place. "Okay. See that archway up there? When we get to the arch, we're going to jump!"

"Jump?" Castor's voice rattled. "Jump where?"

Ripley pointed. "JUMP UP AND GRAB THE ROPE!"

At the archway, April stood on Molly's shoulders on one side and Mal stood on Jo's shoulders on the other. Strung between them, like a clothesline, was a length of rope.

"JUMP!"

And with that, Castor and Ripley sprang up from the mass of moon moles, catching the rope, in Castor's case, with her tail.

The moon moles, unaware, motored on in a cloud of dust.

"Holy Althea Gibson, that was close," Molly huffed, holding April's ankles.

"WHOO HOO!" Ripley yipped, swinging around the rope.

"EASY EASY!" Mal called out, gripping the side of the arch tightly with her sort-of-free hand. "RIPLEY, the rope is attached to us!"

"WHOOPS!" Ripley somersaulted down onto the ground and threw her hands in the air. "RESCUE COMPLETE!"

Castor dropped down after her, landing lightly on her hind legs. "Thank you. Thank you so much."

"Now THAT," April said, re-coiling her rope, "is what you call some pretty serious Lumberjane teamwork in ACTION!"

Molly looked at Castor. Castor was looking at her new vest. "Are you okay?" Molly asked her.

Castor gave a teeny tiny nod, brushing the dust off her fur.

"What was that?" Mal gasped.

Castor sighed. "They're moon moles."

Mal nodded. "Okay. Sure. Moon moles. That makes . . . sense?"

"Do you know why moon moles broke into our cabin?" Jo asked.

"Yeah, and why they would want to carry you away all cartoon style?" April added.

Castor looked at the ground. "They're just doing what they're told."

Molly reached out and put her hand on Castor's back. "Told by who, Castor?"

"My mother."

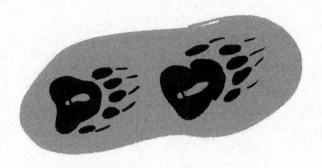

CHAPTER 23

Rosie sat on her porch, a frothy nettle milkshake with honey in one hand, a copy of *The Awesome Power of Famous Redheads in History* in the other. It was nice to have a moment to reflect and relax, a rarity when you are the director of a place like Miss Qiunzella Thiskwin Penniquiqul Thistle Crumpet's camp for Hardcore Lady-Types.

At any camp, on any occasion, a director is always putting out fires. Rosie hadn't put out any fires that day, but she was holding a variety of strings and managing many boiling pots and had also spent the morning tracking down a creature that will be of significance later.

A very large creature.

So it was nice, that evening, to have a moment to look at the stars, to sip a beverage, to consider the mysteries of the

universe and whatnot. Of course, it was going to be short lived, but it's important to enjoy these things while you ca—

"Well, this is another fine mess your scouts have gotten into!" said a growly voice from the blackness just beyond the cabin.

"Good evening to you too, you old COOT," Rosie said, taking a sip of her shake, savoring the nettle-y taste. "Care to expand on that?"

"When I was a director, there was no need to expand on anything." A set of thick brown paws and a scruffy looking bear face stepped forward from the darkness, toward the porch, transforming in a puff of sparkle into the knobby hands and gnarled face of none other than the figure known as Bearwoman.

Although, as Rosie knew, that wasn't her actual name.

"Times have changed," Rosie sighed. "Care to share your concerns?"

"HUMPH, concerns?" Bearwoman pushed her hands onto her hips. "I'm not CONCERNED. I just happened to be out in the woods doing something that's none of your business, and I noticed a small army of moon moles huffing about in the dark. Lost as usual. I thought you should know, as camp director."

Moon moles are not known for their sense of direction on land. A moon mole will happily burrow its way through the core of a planet before asking for directions to the store.

Not that a moon mole has any use for a store. They'd rather pillage than buy.

Rosie raised an eyebrow. "Moon moles, you say."

"Moon moles I DO say," Bearwoman huffed, glaring from behind the thick panes of her very thick spectacles. "And what do you plan to DO about that?"

Rosie stood up. "I will speak to my scouts."

"You know that moon moles means more than just moon moles."

Rosie did know this.

Moon moles are like pancakes and maple syrup, like Jo and April.

One went with the other. In this case, moon moles went with trouble.

"Oh yes," Rosie said.

"Then I guess you've got a handle on it, as usual." Bearwoman's voice dripped with what served as sarcasm for a woman who was also a bear.

And with that, Bearwoman stepped back into the darkness and disappeared into the night, leaving Rosie with a problem to solve.

PART
THREE

RIDDLE ME THIS

"Smack-Dab in the Riddle"

For a Lumberjane, life is full of problems—and solutions.

Some problems, like floods or fires, are physical, and others, like riddles, are a matter of the mind.

The key is to remember that for every problem there is a solution, just as every solution comes with a problem.

The goal is to know what kind of problem you are facing and what is required to solve it. Is it a math problem? Will it require a calculator, slide ruler, or protractor?

Or is it a problem where the solution will involve cunning and concentration, an awareness of all the possibilities at play, some of which will present themselves quickly and others only when . . .

CHAPTER 24

The next morning, Jo slipped out of the cabin before anyone was awake. She stepped out into the early-morning sun, onto the grass covered in glittery pearls of morning dew.

The letter weighed heavily in her pocket. It was quiet, possibly because it was tired out after going on all night, repeating the same argument over and over like a radio ad:

S.T.A.A.R. TODAY! SCIENTIST TOMORROW! YOU KNOW IT'S YOUR DESTINY.

It was getting louder every day.

I'm getting louder, the letter insisted, because you know I'm right, Jo.

Jo?

"Jo?"

Jo swiveled and saw Castor standing in the grass. "Sorry to interrupt."

"Oh." Jo dropped her hands by her sides. "You're not. I just. I'm just walking. Nowhere."

"For fun?" Castor asked.

"Uh." Jo looked at her feet. "No, actually."

"I don't suppose you would fancy a boat ride?" Castor asked.

"Oh." Jo shrugged. "Sure, why not?"

At the dock, Jo held up an oar. "Rowboat okay?"

"Sure," Castor said. "I'm curious to see how this 'oar' functions to move a craft like this on one of your lakes."

"There aren't lakes in Saskatchewan?"

There are many Lumberjane badges available relating to boat safety and nautical awareness (including: Naval Gauging, Keepin' It Reel, and Seal of Approval, to name just a few). Also, being on water in a craft designed to float on water is just really fun, as long as you are SAFE and wearing a life preserver.

Jen would want to add that.

WEAR YOUR LIFE PRESERVER.

Jo found a preserver that didn't completely engulf Castor, and the two of them pushed a small rowboat out onto the lake, which that day was clear and blue and sparkling.

While Jo rowed, Castor gripped the edge of the boat with her claws and leaned over to look at the water. She reached down and stuck a tiny claw into the lake, cutting through the surface with no more pressure than a three-eyed water skater.

At first it was quiet; just the sound of Castor and Jo, little fishes swimming, the bow of the boat cutting smoothly through the still waters of the lake.

Toward the middle of the lake, Castor turned to face Jo.

"I have to tell you something," Castor said. "Actually, I have to tell you all. I told Ripley last night and, well, you're awake, I thought I might as well tell you too."

"Okay," Jo said.

"I'm not here on vacation," Castor said, plainly. "And I'm not from Saskatchewan."

"Sure," Jo said, unsurprised.

Castor sat up, shoving her preserver to the side so she could look at Jo. "I'm a moon pirate."

It is one thing to find out someone is not from Saskatchewan. It's quite another to find out they're a moon pirate.

Jo wasn't sure what she was expecting Castor, a well-dressed talking mouse, to reveal out there in the middle of the lake. It wasn't "I'm a moon pirate."

"You sail through space?" Jo clarified, in case by "moon" Castor meant some parallel dimension or something.

Castor nodded. "On the great ship *Luna*, the ship of my mother, Captain Elara. We sail the skies my ancestors have sailed for millennia."

The next obvious question, if you were Jo, was HOW do you sail through space?

There is a book on this subject, actually, in the Lumberjanes library. It is very old and almost completely stuck together with moon dust. It is bound in silver-tinted leather and tucked under the dictionary of celestial nautical terminology and a map that hasn't been examined for many centuries.

In this book is a complex diagram describing ships like Castor's ship, *Luna*, and how they fly, although several key components are missing, details that reveal how a ball of light can house several hundred mice and move through space at the speed of sound, involving the connection between celestial light and kinetic energy.

Castor did her best to explain to Jo exactly how moonship flight was accomplished, which Jo stored in the back of her brain in a file labeled, "TO DO."

"So, of all the camps in all the galaxies, how is it you ended up here?" Jo asked.

"I'm sorry to say," Castor admitted, looking at her paws, "I was sent to pillage your larders."

"Pillage," Jo said. "I mean, I guess that's kind of a pirate-y thing."

"'Tis THE pirate-y thing," Castor admitted.

Jo considered. "But you didn't . . . pillage. Did you?"

"No," Castor said. "Well, not after that little bit of delicious Alaskan Hybrid."

"But you're not going to take any more?" Jo asked.

"No."

"So then," Jo dipped her oar in the lake, "what happens now?"

"The first bit has already happened," Castor noted.

"Moon moles?" Jo wondered.

"Moon moles." Castor nodded. "Sent to retrieve me after my failed excursion."

"Which I suppose means you can't just stay and enjoy some time at camp," Jo added.

Castor shook her head. "I am the daughter of the captain, which means that I will be captain one day. I have a ship. I have responsibilities. A pirate's life is not really designed for indulgences and . . . fun."

In the corner of the lake, a flock of early-rising scouts was practicing what looked like a synchronized swimming routine that the lake's trout were finding, in two words, "very amusing."

Jo looked down at her hands. "I get that."

"Still," Castor said, leaning over the boat and staring at the reflection of her sad mouse face in the calm, glassy finish of the lake. "I'm glad I got a little fun. It was . . . fun."

"I'm glad you did too," Jo said, pressing the letter in her coat pocket.

"Thank you for the boat ride," Castor said.

"No problem," Jo said. "And I'm sorry. I mean, I'm sorry you have to go."

"I am too." Castor returned to her perch at the front of the boat, tucking her nose into the front of her life jacket.

A dark cloud curled itself over the sun, turning the lake from blue to gray.

On shore, Rosie was waiting.

CHAPTER 25

Jen paced Rosie's cabin, bleary eyed, her hair full of glitter and her eyes drained of sleep. The rest of Roanoke watched as Jen paced, noting that they had never seen anyone who had not slept in as many days as Jen had not slept.

Jen had not slept since . . .

How long had she been working nonstop on Galaxy Wars?

"Jen's moving, like, really fast," said April, with a bit of admiration, because April aspired to be one of the busiest, most efficient people on the planet.

"Jen needs tea," Molly said.

"Jen needs SLEEP," Jo said.

Bubbles chirped in the affirmative. Bubbles loved many

things, and curling up for a snooze was on the top of the list.

Mal couldn't think of what Jen needed yet, but her accordion test was only a day away, and she was still pretty confident that once she passed, everything would go back to normal.

Whatever that was.

"Jerry," Rosie said, "I'm going to need you to take a deep breath."

"Well, it's JEN," Jen muttered, plastering her hands to the sides of her face. "Okay so it's JEN. And. What's happening? Something is happening? There's a mouse? I knew that! Is something else falling apart? Is GALAXY WARS falling apart? Is something wrong?"

"Everything is fine," Rosie said, gently pushing Jen down into a comfy chair, where Jen rocked dangerously close to the cliff of sleep. "We just have the small issue of our newest visitor and the impending arrival of . . ."

"My mother," Castor said.

"Indeed," Rosie said. "Anything else we should know?"

"She was expecting quite a bit of cheese," Castor said. "So she could arrive a bit . . . cranky."

"Well, that we will have to deal with when the time comes," Rosie said, "as we're all pretty fond of our cheese over here."

"Castor's mom's a pirate," Ripley whispered to Mal and Molly.

"That's freaking cool," Mal whispered back.

"Castor is also a pirate," Jo added, in case that wasn't clear.

"Wait. How long have you known Castor was a pirate?" April growled.

"Not very long," Jo said. "Maybe a few thousand seconds."

Jen startled straight, almost knocking her mug to the floor. "FFtah! What? I'm ready! I'm—" She promptly collapsed back asleep.

"So basically, we're thinking your mother will arrive, and you will head back off into the great celestial yonder," Rosie said. "Which I don't think should interrupt Galaxy Wars."

Jen, if she had been awake, would have been relieved. But Jen was in a sleep so deep a herd of elephants could not rouse her.

Ripley stepped forward. "I think Castor should get to participate in Galaxy Wars," she said. "If she has to leave, she should get a chance to play."

"Do you want to play?" Rosie asked.

"Oh, I wouldn't dream," Castor blushed, "of interrupting—"

Rosie leaned on her desk. "I think it's a fine idea. BUT, your cabin will have to decide whose place you'll be taking. You need to compete with the same number you had at the competition's start. Those are the rules, arcane though they may be."

Rosie picked up a blanket and walked over to drop it on Jen, who was curled up like a cat now. "I'll let you choose, and you can let me know tonight."

CHAPTER 26

Y ou don't have to do this," Castor protested, as the members of Roanoke gathered at a picnic bench outside Rosie's cabin. "I came here to steal cheese. I don't deserve your generosity."

"You came here as a pirate to pillage," Jo reminded her. "It's not like you were picking on us or anything."

"Context is everything," Molly agreed.

"Totally," Mal added. "Plus I'm totally messing up lately, so I shouldn't even compete. You should take my spot!"

"Hold on," Molly said, putting her hands on her hips. "Mal, you are awesome. You're our strategist. You should totally play!"

Mal shook her head. "I'm the musician, or I was. JO is the brains, APRIL is the guts, RIPLEY is the muscle," she pointed at Molly, "YOU'RE the heart. You don't need me!"

"First of all, why are we all body parts," April asked. "Second of all, if anything Ripley is the guts. THIRD OF ALL (finally), *of course* we need you, Mal!"

"I'm the one who messed up last time," Jo said, shoving her hands in her pockets. "I mean, I really want us to win because . . ." she looked over at April, sputtered, "but maybe I shouldn't . . ."

"What is going on with you?" April threw her hands in the air. "You're all Billy Jean King about this, which is weird. Like, why do you suddenly care about winning EVEN MORE THAN ME! And now you're like, 'I don't want to play'?!"

149

"If we want to win I shouldn't play," Mal repeated.

"There has to be a solution to this," Jo said. "Maybe if we gave each other basic scores from one to five on different skill sets . . ."

It was a swirl, a hurricane, of Roanoke STRESS. Castor clutched her tail to her chest.

Ripley jumped up on the table. "HEY!!!"

"LISTEN!" she cried, her finger pointed in the air.

"Yes, Rip?" Jo said.

"I have something to say." Ripley put her hands on her hips, her feet braced apart, and whipped her blue hair from her eyes. "And now I'm going to say it."

"Okay!" Roanoke responded in unison.

"The thing I have to say is," Ripley said, looking at her fellow scouts with a twinkly stare, "IT DOESN'T MATTER."

"What doesn't matter?" Mal asked.

"Who wins," Ripley said. "Or winning. Or winning things. Or getting stuff. It doesn't matter. Because we all just want to HAVE FUN. That's the whole point of being a LUMBERJANE. We're supposed to have FUN."

Everyone was quiet. Possibly some of the scouts were scanning their vague recollections of the Lumberjanes pledge to see if the word "fun" was actually mentioned.

"So the person not playing doesn't matter because it doesn't matter if we win so maybe we can draw straws so that everyone but one person gets to have fun and the person . . . not playing can have FUN watching." Ripley finished. And, with a flourish, she took a bow.

The word *FUN* is not explicitly in the Lumberjanes pledge (please refer to page vii), but it's still pretty important.

"Holy Buffy Sainte-Marie," April gasped.

"Ripley is the brains," Mal said.

"Ripley is the whole package," Molly said.

April turned and stood up on her toes so she could be eye to eye with her best friend. "Jo. I think you think I only want to win, and I do want to win but that's not the most important thing to me. You are."

Jo bit her lip.

April turned and looked at Ripley. "Fun is important. And us being a team and having fun TOGETHER is important. And I can't wait to watch you guys."

Jo frowned. "Watch?"

April nodded. "I'm going to cheer you on, and you're going to have an AMAZING TIME. And I'll have an amazing time because you guys are awesome."

Taking Jo's hand, April leaned in and whispered, "And when you're ready to tell me what's been bugging you for the past four days, I'm here."

For once, the letter was silent.

CHAPTER 27

The Final Event. The result of endless amounts of blood, sweat, and tears rose up from the field, a true achievement of obstacle wonder.

The event all had been waiting for with bated breath.

It was THE INTERGALACTIC WARRIOR SPECTACLE OBSTACLE EXTRAVAGANZA, consisting of walls, ropes, tunnels, drops, balls, bouncing, and other necessary camp games sections.

Jen, after sleeping for six hours in what looked to Rosie like a stone-cold coma, was a new woman, glowing like a pulsar on its first birthday. She radiated glee, bounding around in front of the starting line with her megaphone and her little moon hat.

"THE STANDINGS ARE ZODIAC IN FIRST,

ROANOKE IN SECOND, WOOLPIT IN THIRD! BUT NO MATTER WHAT YOUR PLACE, I WANT YOU TO GO OUT THERE AND HAVE FUN!"

The scouts cheered ravenously.

"AAAARRRRRREEE YOOOOOOOUUUUU REAAAADYYY!!!?????"

The cabins lined up on the line, game faces ON.

Dartmoor had color-coordinated black jumpsuits with little stars sewn on the backs. Woolpit had managed matching moon-embellished tank tops. Zodiac were all wearing what looked like astronaut uniforms, stitched together by Barney.

"We're going to win," Wren from Zodiac growled.

"Heck ya," Hes hollered, with a solid high five to Barney.

Barney, who was still wearing their star, turned and waved at Roanoke. "GOOD LUCK!"

"YOU TOO!" Roanoke waved back in unison.

Roanoke had opted to liberally plaster their faces with glitter, in honor of team captain RIPLEY!

"I've already breathed in like a cup of it," Molly admitted.

"We'll have the sparkliest lungs in the universe," Mal coughed.

April, true to form, was ready to cheer for TEAM ROANOKE with every drop of her might.

153

"YEAH! YOU CAN DO IT! YEAH! GOOOOOO, TEAM!"

Next to April, Bubbles cartwheeled and back-flipped with excitement.

"SQUEEEAK! SQUEEEAK!"

"Okay, team," Ripley said, jogging in place. "Remember the most important thing today is the most important thing always and that is?"

"HAVE FUN!" everyone screamed back in chorus.

Even the creatures of the forest gathered to watch what seemed like something of a crazy spectacle for such an hour.

"So," a frizzy-haired fox wondered aloud. "This is like a competition? For food?"

"I heard there was pizza," a hedgehog replied. "I would do this for pizza."

"Yes, yes," a grumpy bear replied. "Now hush up so we can watch."

"ALL RIGHT, SCOUTS." Jen stood at the front of the starting line. "ON YOUR MARTA!"

"GET SAVITRI!"

"GLORIA!"

The scouts sprinted forward in a massive herd of shouting, yipping, thundering scouts, dropping to their knees to wiggle through the first obstacle, a set of tunnels: CRAWL THROUGH THE BLACK HOLE!

Castor skipped through easily, as did Ripley.

"Come on, team!" Ripley called down the tube.

"This is so fabulous," Castor squeaked excitedly.

"Why. Small. Tube," Jo huffed, twisting her body left and right while Molly did her best to caterpillar through, and Mal crawled using a combination of fingers and toes.

Next. FOLLOW THE MILKY WAY! A giant constellation of white ropes was laid out on top of a set of ladders, which scouts had to climb up onto then tightrope across or end up in a moon pool of freezing water.

Castor raced across the ropes, her little claws dancing over them like she'd done it a million times before.

Safely on the other side, Ripley turned to her team.

"Why. Always. Water?" Mal shivered, doing her best not to look down.

"Okay," Ripley said, once they'd all made it across, "to make this next leg more fun, I have an idea. Okay?"

Jo grinned. "I'm down."

Mal and Molly and Castor nodded.

Zodiac team turned back to see Castor and Ripley and Mal and Molly and Jo pretend to be floating in zero gravity to their next obstacle, laughing hysterically.

"What are they doing?" Skulls giggled.

"They're moon walking," Hes sighed.

"They're slowing down," Wren frowned.

"Whatever," Hes said. "If they don't wanna win, we'll win."

After that, Team Roanoke completed the SOLAR SWING and headed to the GAH-STRONOMY section, where Roanoke dutifully shoved a handful of crackers in their mouths and whistled, a task that made Molly laugh so hard she shot cracker out of her nose, which made Mal laugh so hard SHE shot cracker out of her nose.

They made a five-scout human ladder to get over the ON TOP OF THE WORLD obstacle, a seven-foot-high wall, with Castor scampering up and over first, so she could help Ripley pull up Mal and Molly.

"GO TEAM ROANOKE!" April screamed, running along the side of the course.

"SQUEEEAK!" Bubbles cheered from April's shoulders.

"YOUR LAST CHALLENGE," Jen called out through the megaphone, "IS 'OVER THE MOON!' YOU MUST KEEP YOUR MOON IN ORBIT AS YOU RACE ACROSS THE FIELD TO THE FINISH LINE!"

"Ready?" Ripley grabbed a large white ball from the stack.

"Ready!" Jo called back, stepping onto the field.

"IF THE BALL DROPS, YOU MUST RETURN TO THE EDGE OF THE FIELD AND START AGAIN."

Ripley volleyed the volleyball up and into the air.

"GOT IT!" Castor gave it a solid bop with her tail.

"GOT IT!" Jo backhanded it over to Molly, who popped it back into the air for Mal.

"You know," Mal said, punching the ball in Jo's direction, "this seems oddly do-able."

"I know," Molly said. "I feel like at any moment a herd of angry sheep could ride out onto the field and attack us with Wiffle bats or something."

"Or," Mal said, spotting the volleyball again, "could it be that the end of this race is in sight?"

Molly wanted to say, "Nah, too easy," but saying "too easy" is like looking around for something hard to do.

Ripley gave the ball an extra-hard punt and it shot, with a whistle, straight up into the air.

Everyone looked up to see where it would fall.

"What," Molly asked.

"Is," Mal continued.

"That?" Jo marveled.

Castor looked up and sighed. "Barnacles."

Up in the sky, a shadow blackened the center of the moon, accompanied, as shadows like this are, with a whooshing and a *thhp thhp thhp*, the sound of something cutting through the air—the sound of flight.

It was a familiar sound if you were a moon mouse. Castor's little pink ears quivered.

The volleyball came to a soft landing on the ground, on the otherwise empty field. Jo, Mal, Molly, and Ripley ignored it as they watched the shadow get bigger and bigger and bigger.

Closer, closer, and closer.

April crept to the edge of the field. "What the Octavia E. Butler?"

Just then, the earth shook. A wall of moon moles burrowed up from the ground, their pink noses pushing back the earth as they pulled themselves up to form a wall around the field, trapping Roanoke inside.

"Oh no, you don't!" April charged and vaulted over the emerging moon mole barrier to her team.

"What's happening?" she shouted over the din of digging claws and screeching shadows.

Castor sighed. "Mother's here."

CHAPTER 28

On Parents' Day, parents and guardians are invited to join scouts in a series of activities to highlight scouts' accomplishments and goals.

On this day, parents take a narrow road through the woods, which leads through the archway entrance to the main campus.

Castor's mother, Captain Elara, dropped in out of the sky, after traveling a great distance along what Moon Pirates refer to as the great intergalactic current, on the great ship *Luna*.

The *Luna* was not your average vessel. It was built for moon voyages and moon mice, and it was light and quick for banking past stars. Inside it was full of gears and levers perfect for little paws, compartments for eating and sleeping and flying, and . . . well that's about it really. Outside it was roughly the size of a treehouse, but round, perfectly round, and glowing, a globe of quivering light with a whirring, spinning surface, a surface made up of a number of mechanics that would blow the average mechanic's mind.

It was a moon-shaped vessel built for traveling from moon to moon to moon, in search of whatever was available, preferably cheese, a substance more plentiful than most people would think and most cheese lovers would dare to dream.

The *Luna* landed on the field with a massive whoosh of air, a wave that sent the scouts on the field toppling backward into the wall of moles standing guard.

As Roanoke scrambled to their feet, there was another whirring noise. From inside the glow and between the spinning parts of the ship's flying gears, a large door popped open with a blast of what looked like bluish fog.

Out fanned a small army of mice in fine silk coats and leather belts, all carrying little silver swords, followed by the great captain herself.

Captain Elara was a relatively tall, broad-shouldered, and long-tailed mouse. She wore gold and silver rings on her claws and around her tail. Her long, gold petticoat was thickly embroidered and bedazzled with gemstones. Even her whiskers were tinted silver and gold. On her head

perched a large pear-shaped hat with a feather sticking straight out of the top.

"Great jewels of Jupiter, Mother," Castor scampered forward, "it's not that formal a planet. You needn't be so ceremonial."

Captain Elara was not amused. "I beg your pardon?" She stomped her paw, rattling her rings. "You dare to 'Great jewels of Jupiter, Mother' *me* after you have failed quite miserably at retrieving even a slice of cheese from this miserable planet stocked with Swiss-brained fools?"

Castor crossed her paws over her chest. "These people are my friends! I refuse to pillage from them."

The feather on Elara's hat bobbed as she fumed. "HON-ESTLY, CASTOR! What are you, a MOUSE or a HUMAN?"

"I am a mouse," Castor said. Then, quietly, "And you needn't be so rude."

"Uh, hi." Jo stepped forward, smiling hospitably. "I'm Jo, member of Roanoke cabin, uh, heh, human. I'm usually the one who does introductions. These are my fellow scouts Mal, Molly, Ripley, and April."

"Hi." They all waved nervously.

"So." Jo considered the best approach, having never spoken to a moon pirate before. "We just wanted to say that we've had an amazing time with Castor, and we think she's really smart and she would make a great scout."

Captain Elara flicked her jeweled tail and snorted. "SCOUT?" she sneered. "SCOUT? BLASPHEMOUS! Castor is a PIRATE!"

The row of pirates behind her nodded in unison.

"A PIRATE," Elara's jewels shook, "is a serious occupation!"

The row of pirates nodded again.

"Hear, hear," one squeaked.

"Ahem," Jo coughed.

"You humans wouldn't know anything about it," Captain Elara grumbled. "Frittering your days away. The CHEESE is WASTED on you."

April looked at Jo. "Yeek."

"Castor, you get your tail on board that ship right now," Elara said, pointing with a ringed paw at the *Luna.* "I've had it up to my hat with this nonsense."

Castor turned back to her adopted cabin. "I can't apologize enough," she said, in a low squeak. "Thank you so much for everything. Thank you for the vest, Ripley. I had . . . fun. Really."

Ripley sniffed and waved. "Bye, Castor."

And with that, Castor turned and padded past her mother and toward the ship, ears pressed against her head, through the line of mice lined up outside the ship, all tut-tutting.

"Great Neptune and all its ice formations, Castor, where is your coat?" Elara frowned, watching Castor go. "Is that DENIM?"

"It's no fair," Ripley said, her chin pressed to her chest. "We were just starting to have fun."

There once was a scout who only knew what she wanted to eat when it was on someone else's plate. Which was annoying, but sometimes it is easier to see things clearly when they are outside yourself, walking a long, sad walk onto an otherwise miraculous piece of machinery.

Jo pressed her lips together.

Castor, she thought, *should not have to leave.*

Who said being a scout didn't have some connection to something as awesome as destiny?

No one Jo had heard of.

Actually, the letter began, if we're talking about greatness and how to get there, which it seems we are . . .

But Jo was not listening.

"You know what? Fun is important," Jo said to herself, stepping forward. "FUN. IS. IMPORTANT. TOO."

"CAPTAIN ELARA!" Jo shouted.

"Oh, WHAT IS IT NOW?" Captain Elara snapped, flustered.

Jo stood straight and tall. "I think Castor should be allowed to stay. I think being allowed to have a little fun is more important than you think. I think fun . . ."

April bit her lip.

Ripley beamed.

"Is awesome." Jo finished.

Captain Elara waved her hand at Jo, as though trying to wave her away. "Castor is destined for serious things. She needs to focus on serious things. This is no place for a future captain."

"I think you're wrong," Jo said. "I think this is exactly where Castor should be."

"Oh, do you now?" Captain Elara smiled, revealing a diamond-studded set of front teeth. "How much are you willing to wager on it?"

CHAPTER 29

Of the battles a Lumberjane will face, a battle of wits is perhaps the most important. (One of the longest battles of wits in Lumberjanes history took place over a decade and involved two scouts, one of whom is currently known as Bearwoman.

Over the years, it was often unclear as to who was winning this battle of wits, or even who was still playing.

In the end, the battle was won with four simple words: "I told you so."

I won't say who won, as winning, as we've said, is not necessarily as important as having fun.)

Anyway.

A battle of wits is a battle without weapons. It is a battle of brains.

And not even book brains, but thinking brains.

A thinking brain can go anywhere and do anything.

A thinking brain is a valuable thing.

Captain Elara knew this. As did Jo.

"If I can solve your riddle, and you can't solve mine," Jo proposed, "Castor stays."

"Indeed. And if I can solve yours, and you cannot solve mine . . ." Elara ran a claw over a long, golden whisker, "Castor leaves AND you all hand over YOUR ENTIRE LARDER OF CHEESE."

Mal whistled.

"No tacos, no pizza, no enchiladas, no grilled cheese for the rest of the summer." Ripley gulped.

"Double yeek," Mal added.

"If only we were lactose intolerant and didn't care about such things," April sighed.

"We gotta do it," Ripley said. "We just gotta."

Everyone nodded vigorously. YES.

"Watch out," Castor said, darting over to whisper. "My mother is renowned across the universe for her riddling skills. She once made the regal Dauphin of Neptune cry when she beat him four out of five."

"We're in," Jo announced, standing tall in front of her cabin. "Captains first."

"Very well." Standing in front of her ship, the great Captain Elara posed two of her crew side by side.

She clapped her jeweled paws together twice and each mouse assumed a guard's stiff stance, swords pointed into the ground, chins up, ears back, and eyes staring straight ahead.

"Standing before you are two mice guarding two doors," the captain began. "One mouse guards the door to cheese. The other mouse guards the door to the place where there is never cheese."

"That's not Gouda," April said quietly.

"The mouse guarding the door to cheese will always tell the truth, and the mouse guarding the door to the place where there is never cheese will always lie. BUT! In appearance, they are indistinguishable."

The two mice synchronously spun their swords and stared grimly forward.

Captain Elara stepped toward Roanoke, her claw outstretched. "You may ask either guard ONE QUESTION and ONE QUESTION ONLY to discover the door leading to cheese. THEN you must tell me which door you chose."

"Right," Jo said, turning to the rest of the scouts. "Thoughts?"

Molly took Mal's hand. "What do you think?"

Mal shook her head. "I can't think. I just need to pass my badge. After that I can do this."

"You can do it now," Molly insisted, pulling Mal into a hug. "Mal, you're awesome at music AND you like solving puzzles AND you're funny."

Mal blushed. "I'm funny?"

Molly smiled. "And you have really cool style."

Mal turned and looked at the two mice. Then she turned back to Molly. "I thought I was good at music. I was wrong."

Molly grabbed Mal by the shoulders and squeezed her tight. "You weren't wrong," she said. "'Bohemian Rhapsody' is a really hard song."

And with that Molly placed a very tiny kiss on the tip of Mal's nose.

"Aw." April smiled.

"Come on, Mal," Jo said. "You can do this."

Mal stepped forward. Looked at one mouse. Then the other.

Suddenly, Mal smiled a big toothy Mal smile. The kind of smile that lights up a room like a light bulb or a lightning strike.

"I've got it," she said.

Mal turned to the mouse on the right. "If I ask the other mouse which door leads to cheese, which door would they point to?"

The mouse frowned. "The other mouse would say that the door behind me goes to cheese."

Mal turned back, beaming. "That's it!" she said, bouncing up and down. "No matter what the answer, the door that gets pointed to will lead to the place with no cheese! The lying mouse will LIE and point to the door that DOESN'T lead to cheese. The honest mouse will tell the truth and point to the door that the lying mouse would say leads to cheese, which will lead to a place where there is never cheese. So no matter what, it's the other door."

One of Ripley's eyes got really big. "Uhhhhhh."

"That sounds right to me," Jo said.

"Provolone it." April grinned.

"It's this door," Mal said, pointing to the door on the left.

The mouse on the left bowed low. "Madam is correct."

"Well done," Captain Elara sniffed. "But I warn you, fooling me will NOT be easy."

CHAPTER 30

H ow is this even a fair contest?" Captain Elara drawled. "A clump of scouts facing off against me, the captain, well versed in all manner of academics, tried and tested by years on the celestial seas. I don't know if you know that I made the Dauphin cry once many moons ago."

"We heard," Ripley said. "Poor Dauphin."

"This had better be good." Molly bit her lip.

Jo pressed her finger to her lips.

As sometimes happens when you do this, Jo's brain was suddenly pinged with a memory, an answer to a question she'd forgotten she'd even asked.

"Hey," she said, turning to April. "I just remembered the name of our favorite game."

April looked up. "Which game?"

"Remember we were talking in the cabin, about games from when we were kids?" Jo smiled. "THE MOON IS UP!"

"Oh my AMY POEHLER, THAT'S IT!" April grabbed Jo's arm and started jumping up and down.

"For this riddle," Jo said, turning to Captain Elara, "we will all kneel in a circle."

The mice looked at Captain Elara, confused.

"Just do it," Captain Elara sighed, twisting her hand in the air like a bored windmill.

"All of us," April said, running forward and herding the mice into a large ring. "Come on, don't be shy."

Once they had all assembled, Jo took a saber from one of the mice and held it in the air. "Today we are going to play a Lumberjane classic, THE MOON IS UP. It is required of all playing to correctly place the sabre so that the MOON IS UP."

Jo took her spot kneeling with the rest of the campers. "You have one round to figure it out, Captain," she said. "And so . . ."

Jo held up the sabre high. "THE MOON," she called, leaning forward and placing the sabre on the grass in front of her, "IS UP."

April took the sabre next. She held it even higher. "THE

MOOOOOON!" she trilled, placing the sabre down so that her chin was almost on the ground. "IS UP!"

The mice watched in confusion, twitching whiskers and tails, sniffing the air curiously.

"The MOON!" Mal picked up the sabre, spun it several times, and placed it on the ground, pointed to the left. "IS UP."

One of the mice took the sabre and placed it on the ground. "The moon is up?"

"The moon is not up," Jo said solemnly.

Another burly mouse with black stripes on his ears and a

gold coat grabbed the sabre. "GIVE ME THAT." He placed it on the ground, crouching. "The moon is up?"

"The moon is up!" Ripley cheered.

"HO HO!" The mouse chortled, smiling hopefully at his captain. "The captain will surely win now."

"This makes about as much sense as a moon mole cartwheel," Captain Elara huffed.

It all looked the same from where Elara was standing. Some mice put the sabre down lengthwise, some longwise. That didn't seem to affect whether the moon was up. Putting the sabre down soft or with a thud didn't matter, either. One mouse yelled THE MOON IS UP and the other whispered. And in both cases, the moon was not up.

"What is this ridiculous game?" Captain Elara snarled, her diamond teeth flashing.

"All games require skill," Jo noted. "Skills come in all shapes and sizes."

"Like pies," Ripley added. "And cupcakes. And swimsuits."

"See if you can do it," April said, gesturing to the ground.

"Humph." The Captain gently lowered herself to her knees and took the sabre in hand. She held the sabre high in the sky, "The moon is up!"

Still kneeling, she placed the sword on the ground.

Jo shook her head. "The moon is not up."

"Well, it's completely barnacle." Captain Elara scrambled to her feet.

"I think I have it," Castor said, stepping toward the circle and taking the sabre.

Kneeling on the ground, Castor placed the sword in front of her. Jutting her tail up into the air, she cried, "The moon is up!"

"That's right!" Jo whistled.

"HO HO HO! I've got it! It's the sabre!" Captain Elara proclaimed, snatching the sabre from Castor's paws. "The sabre must be pointing at the moon. Victory is mine!"

"Nope." Castor grabbed the sword back and placed it on the ground, crouching forward. "You've lost, Mother. The moon is your bottom. When your tail is up, the moon is up."

"That," Captain Elara sniffed, "is disgusting."

"Yeah it's kind of an off-color example of camp humor," Jo admitted. "But, all the same, we win."

"HA HA!" Ripley grabbed Castor by the arms and swung her around gleefully. "WE WIN WITH FUN!"

"We won with butts!" Mal cheered.

"YAY BUTTS!" Molly whooped.

Ripley jumped up in a full shooting star. "CASTOR STAYS!"

CHAPTER 31

It was a curiously peaceful day at Miss Qiunzella Thiskwin Penniquiqul Thistle Crumpet's camp for Hardcore Lady-Types.

An assortment of birds sang from their perches in the pines of the forest.

It was the first day after Castor's last day at camp. Her mother had agreed to let her stay for two orbits, which is about six days of Lumberjane time.

Six days turned out to be enough time for Castor to complete her Sew Be It badge, as well as her View to a Kiln badge, and it turned out she was a natural at stitching and pottery, both. She also took her Will You Weave Mine badge, making a little moon-shaped carpet for Roanoke cabin, and her Just Bead It badge, during which she enjoyed countless hours stringing tiny glass beads into endless orbits that now decorated almost every cabin.

Castor, it turned out, was a natural crafter, assisted in her beading projects by her nimble and tiny paws.

She even took a That's How the Cookie Crumbles badge with Barney, even though none of the cookies had cheese in them.

It was only six days, Lumberjane time, which is kind of short for a summer, but for Castor it felt like everything. It felt like a lifetime.

Time is a funny thing, Jo thought.

Mal and Molly were now working on their Bang the Drum badges, along with Marcy and Maxine P. from Woolpit, who had emerged as the victors of Galaxy Wars and were all sporting their new fancy space pins.

Thump thump thump thump

Thump thump thump thump

"It's like the rhythm of your body," Kzzyzy, both cook and the drum instructor, explained. "You have to hear your rhythms."

"What do you think about doing Rush's 'La Villa Strangiato' for our badge test?" Mal mused.

"Is it a hard song?" Molly asked.

Mal waggled her hand in the air. "Meh."

Molly squinted. "Okay, but if it's more than five minutes we're picking another song."

BunBun was lying on her back, her suitcase tucked under her head, watching the clouds go by. "FEEL the RHYthm," she chanted. "FEEL the RHYthm."

Jo sat in the grass, thinking.

Only a few days earlier, she had mailed her response to THE CENTER FOR SCIENTIFIC ADVANCEMENT AND RESEARCH.

Esteemed Center Members,

Thank you for your offer to take part in S.T.A.A.R. this summer. I am not currently available to take this position.

But I thank you for the opportunity, and I hope to work with you in the future.

Jo

All the voices in her head were her own now.

It was a welcome relief. Because the voices in Jo's always-thinking, always-analyzing brain were quite enough.

"Greetings, my good friend, my pal, my confidant!" April bounded over and gently sucker-punched Jo in the shoulder. "And what skills are you acquiring at this fine institution on this fine morning?"

"Actually, I'm thinking about something I want to talk to you about," Jo said.

"Oh?" April asked.

Jo sighed, patting the grass next to her. "Sit."

April sat.

"Okay," Jo said. "So. Right when Castor got here, my dads forwarded me this letter, about a summer study program . . . like a science thing . . . which would have meant leaving . . ."

"GAH! HORRORS!" April slapped her hands onto her face and threw her body backward. SHOCK AND DISMAY!

"Yeah," Jo said. "So I was bummed about it. Because I thought it meant that I would HAVE to leave. But then I realized, you know, I came here because I wanted to be here. And that hasn't changed. So I decided just because I COULD go somewhere like that, just because I got in, doesn't mean I have to go. So I chose to stay."

"You still wanna have fun," April grinned. "Because girls just wanna."

"Yeah," Jo nodded. "I do, as Cyndi Lauper suggests, like people of all gender expressions, wanna have fun, and I knew that when I came here this summer, and I know that now. I just had to think about it for a bit."

April lunged forward and locked Jo in a giant April hug, squeezing her as hard as she could squeeze anything.

If she squeezed any harder, Jo would turn into a diamond.

"Don't EVER GO!" she growled. "Never to infinity is when you're allowed to go."

"I'm not going anywhere right now," Jo said, squeezing back, although April was making her right arm a little numb. "Right now, our main job is to be the best Lumberjanes we can be, not to worry about this stuff."

"Quite," April said, finally releasing Jo.

Jo lay back on the grass, enjoying the familiar itchy tickle on her skin. April lay down next to her, still buzzing with an April-esque energy.

"So, I feel like I always ask you what you are thinking about," April said. "And you always say 'stuff' or 'things,' but I know you're thinking about more. And I think it would be educational and inspirational, you know, to hear more of the inner thoughts of Jo."

"Fair," Jo said, grabbing a stalk of grass and lightly nibbling on the end with her teeth.

"So," April said, "lay it on me, what's going on in your head? You know, today?"

"All of it?"

April paused. Reconsidered. "Most of it. Give me eighty-eight percent."

"Okay." Jo took a deep breath. "Today I'm thinking

about space. You know, like, how we can get Lumber-jane badges for stuff to do with outer space . . ."

"Yeah," April said, "although admittedly even I'm taking some SPACE from that for the moment."

"Also," Jo continued, "there's INNER SPACE, which made me think maybe we should all get our Meditate on It badges."

"Not a terrible idea," April said, reaching up her finger to catch a wandering butterfly.

"Also I was thinking about the All over the Map badge, and how you can study the boundaries between different territories and spaces."

"Mmmhmmm." April watched the butterfly settle for a short nap on the tip of her finger and resolved to stay as still as she could for as long as the butterfly would stay there.

"The thing about space is," Jo said, "sometimes it's hard to know where one space ends and the other begins. I mean, yes, you can draw a line and say, 'This is one world, and this is the other,' but that line is just a line someone drew. And who knows why they drew it in the first place. The reality of space is that its limits are often fuzzy. And not just when you're looking through a telescope. Like where does the earth end and the sky begin, you know? Where does Castor's home start and ours stop? The line between worlds is subjective and so unstable, but also movable. I mean, I think a lot of people try to keep worlds separate, but there is not a line between home and here, just space. You know? Particles? And I think that's pretty cool."

"What the quark?! That's what you were thinking about?" April asked. "Like, just sitting there, quietly, you're thinking all that?!"

"That's a few of the many things I'm thinking about," Jo said. "Like maybe eighty-two percent."

"That is entirely impressive," April said. "You are an endlessly, entirely impressive person, Jo."

The butterfly, now rested, beat its wings and soared up and off in the current of the light breeze.

April watched the butterfly float up into the sky. "Isn't there also a theory about how little things can, like, make big things happen? About a butterfly?"

"The Butterfly Effect," Jo said.

"In other news," April popped up and looked around, "where's Ripley?"

Another good question.

Ripley was off in a relatively untouched part of the woods, looking at a very large, very golden egg with wide eyes.

"When you hatch," she cooed, pressing her hand against the shell, "I'm going to call you Doctor Glitterface."

In a more distant part of the woods, Rosie stood inside what could only be described as a ginormous paw print. "Oh my," she said, adjusting her glasses. "This could very well be a thing."

SOME LUMBERJANES BADGES!

GROW UP!
How do YOU make your garden grow? With this badge, Lumberjanes learn the basics of seeds and soil, planting and pruning, all the things you need to know to GO ORGANIC GO GO GO!

ASTRONO-ME-ME-ME
Do you see stars? You will with this badge, which covers everything from pulsars to planets, exploring the great beyond in the night sky.

WOOL YOU BE MINE
Are ewe looking to knit your own? Sheepish about the state of your purl and cable? Join the fun and learn how to knit and crochet your way into fabulousness!

GUITAR IT ON
Joan Jett the revolution! Whether you're fender or acoustic, the guitar is the perfect instrument for the budding young artist. Pick up a guitar and master the chords you need to rock your world.

SEE YOU A WELL-ROUNDED
This badge is for scouts who want to combine skills and expand their horizons in more ways than one. Pull a classic combo or combine unexpected badge abilities and show your unique versatility.

OFF THE HOOK
Take up the craft that rug-hooking fans everywhere have been calling "very enjoyable" for centuries. This badge includes instruction in traditional rug hooking, proddy rug hooking, wool appliqué, and feminist fibrous filigree. Join the fun! Get hooked!

HEY BATTA BATTA!
PLAY BALL: fast balls, curve balls, breaking balls, screwballs, balls, and strikes, it's all covered in this badge that celebrates the great American pastime. What a catch!

575
This badge is for scouts/Want to learn some poetry/Haiku is the best.

BETTER SAFETY THAN SORRY
Prevent forest fires, electrical fires, trips, falls, and a variety of other mishaps and preventable things with this badge for the safety conscious and those who need to be more safety conscious. Safety is a scout's first priority; with this badge you come prepared.

BE SO DRAMATIC
All the world IS a stage! Channel your inner thespian with this badge for scouts looking to EXPRESS THEMSELVES.

TIME AFTER TIME
Tick tock, Lumberjanes! Time flies when you're having fun! Or does it? Also, sundials.

HOSTING FOR THE BEST
The skills of hospitality, for scouts, are more than just etiquette. How do you make your home, or town, or school a place that is welcome to newcomers whenever they arrive and wherever they are from?

SKIP IT
Ice cream, double Dutch, do you like skipping very much? Join the next big thing in things you can do with ropes and jumping. Learn tricks like the Side Swing Cross, the Rock and Roll, the Hot Dog, and the Halperia Side Toe Tap!

RIDDLE ME THIS
Like a play on words? Some mental math? Step into the maze with this badge for scouts who want to know the answer to questions designed to stump you.

JUST BEAD IT
Glass, bone, clay, shell, wood, plastic, and crystal! Strung together by scouts who have received this badge, these little holey bits can become fabulous wearable works of art!

BANG THE DRUM
Get percussive with this badge for scouts who love rhythm.

The Lumberjanes head back to camp
in **BOOK 3: THE GOOD EGG!**
Read on for a sample.

CHAPTER 1

Famous researcher, scientist, and Lumberjane, Miss Jane Petunia Massy Acorn Dale once conducted an extensive study on the phenomenon of human grown-ups.

Jane wanted to understand what it was that made a grown-up a grown-up. To do this, she sought to observe grown-ups. To understand their ways and habits.

It was the only study she ever abandoned, because it was too annoying.

Grown-ups, she wrote in her extensive field notes, often declare that they are grown-up but cannot say why or when this happened. Even when questioned. Also, grown-ups are always quick to point out when someone is not a grown-up. Also, aside from clothing and cars, there is nothing particularly distinctive about grown-ups, compared to not-grown-ups. So they are bigger, Jane noted, so what?

In the end, the study yielded more questions and vague definitions than answers. So Jane went back to her research on birds and animals and felt much better about it.

The woods outside Miss Qiunzella Thiskwin Penniquiqul Thistle Crumpet's Camp for Hardcore Lady-Types have always been fruitful for the study of aviary and mammalian behavior.

On the morning that our story begins, the trees boomed with a cacophony of sounds.

A cacophony is kind of like a buffet of very different noises mixed together, but in a very awkward and loud way. So, really, it's more like how your plate looks after you visit a buffet, if it were possible to pile a plate high with SOUNDS.

In this case, sounds like:

SNNURT!

WHOO WHOO!

WEEEDY WEEEDY WEEEE

CHIT CHIT CCHHHIT

To name just a few.

Cacophonies, like buffets, aren't for everyone.

Some people like a lot of noise; the more noises together, the better.

Some people would just prefer if you would generally keep your voice down.

Lumberjanes tend to fall on the side of people who like noise, partly because noise is a big part of being a Lumberjane. There are cheers scouts like to cheer at dinner and campfire songs for campfire times. Also, there are many badges that specifically reward Lumberjanes for being loud, including: Let Your Trombone Slide, "Hear! Hear!" Give a Cheer, and, of course, the Yodeling badge, YODELA-HEEEWHOOO Wants to Know.

A scout with the WHOOO WHOOOO's Calling badge could have stood in the woods, closed their eyes, and caught the identifying features that make up the calls of wild boars, barn owls, flying squirrels, weasels, titmouses, and the fabulous blue-crested Ripley.

GEK-GGGEK

MURRROOOOOO

Tra la la!

The blue-crested Ripley, who will (you'll see) be the hero of this story, is a human creature and a Lumberjane with a shock of blue hair, a massive appetite, and a preference for orange clothing. Ripleys enjoy bouncing, running, jumping, frolicking, dancing, and singing, sometimes while sitting high up in very large pine trees, as she was on this particular morning.

LA LA LA!

Singing is how Ripleys keep track of things and goings-on and whatnot. Because Ripleys, unlike Aprils or Jos, are not really into writing things down in notebooks and journals.

This, of course, is fine. Because everyone, every creature, is different.

Some scouts like to write things down. Some, like Ripley's very good friend and fellow Roanoke cabin member April, like to write and underline things and draw a picture and write more notes and then highlight the whole thing with a bright yellow highlighter.

Some don't.

For Ripley, writing things down was a very slow process that was very unlike bouncing.

Which Ripley much preferred.

Singing is a little like bouncing. Especially if the song comes from that bouncy castle in your heart.

On this day, Ripley was singing about a mouse named Castor, who was also a Moon Pirate and whose Lumberjane story had come to a close recently, when she climbed back into her space pirate ship and soared up into the sky.

Castor loves cheese, Ripley sang.
And glitter if you please
She lives on a ship
She's taking a trip
To the mooooooon
What else is happening?
Well let's see
Lots of things hap-pen to me
So, also I have found . . .

Ripley flipped her legs up and tipped backward, swing-ing around and grabbing onto the branch. Still holding on with one hand, she dangled down over . . .

. . . a big nest
Of really really really really big golden eggs

Of course, when describing something as big or little, it is worth noting that "big" and "little" are subjective terms, which is to say, one person's notion of BIG could be rela-tively small compared to someone else's. This is most often noted when cake is being served.

Still, most people would have to admit that the nest below Ripley was HUGE. It was as big as a cabin. The eggs, most of the eggs, were as big as Ripley. With one exception.

And a little gold egg that I like best.

Eggie was a smaller, basketball-size egg that Ripley had noticed on the edge of the nest.

"Hello, Eggie," Ripley trilled happily.

A basketball-size egg would probably be considered a big egg if you put it next to the kind of eggs you normally find in nests. If you put it next to a robin's egg—which are so small you can fit three in your hand, depending on how big your hand is—the basketball-size egg would be . . . enormous.

But in its nest surrounded by its massive siblings, Eggie was tiny.

Wee even.

Ripley dropped down from her branch and leaned in close to the nest.

"How are you today, Eggie? Are you egg-cellent?"

Eggs, generally, do not make noise. Yet. They are PRE-noise. So Eggie said nothing. But Ripley liked to say encouraging things to it all the same.

"Anyway," Ripley said, smiling at Eggie, "it was really nice hanging out with you. I gotta go, but I'll see you tomorrow, okay?"

Eggie sat silent.

"Kay, see ya!"

Ripley skipped off to camp, her feet crunching into the forest floor with every step. It was time to go do scout things. The day, and the story of Ripley, was just beginning, and there was much to do.

CHAPTER 2

A happy camp is, among other things, a clean and orderly camp.

Mostly because it's just really annoying to step on something, like a whiffle bat or a rake, when you're not expecting to step on something.

Also, keeping things orderly makes it easier to finish jigsaw puzzles.

As former head counselor Mademoiselle Suzannah Saror Mareng Salamader III once noted, "Everything has a place, and so everything in its place, and if it's not there, that's minus two points."

This was, of course, back when there was a points system.

Which there isn't, anymore.

Currently, the philosophy of Miss Qiunzella Thiskwin Penniquiqul Thistle Crumpet's Camp for Hardcore Lady-Types was: Cleanliness is next to awesomeness.

As part of the GREAT CABIN CLEANUP, the scouts of Roanoke cabin—actually the whole camp, including Dartmoor, Woolpit, Zodiac, Roswell, Dighton, and even Aurora—were cabin cleaning.

Jen, the counselor for Roanoke cabin, stood on the steps in her recently ironed green and yellow uniform with matching clipboard, a newly polished whistle dangling around her neck. Her eyes shone with excitement, and her beret was perfectly angled on the top of her head for maximum beret effect. Jen liked putting things in order.

Cleaning was something Jen enjoyed almost as much as Ripley enjoyed singing or bouncing.

"ALL RIGHT, SCOUTS!" Jen shouted as she marched down the stairs. "I WANT TO SEE ALL THE CLUTTER, ALL THE STUFF, EVERYTHING UNDER YOUR BUNKS, OVER YOUR BUNKS, BETWEEN YOUR BUNKS, ALL THE MESS, CLEANED UP! LET'S GO! LET'S DO THIS!"

April emerged from Roanoke carrying a pile of stuff almost as big as April was, which is about four and a half feet high (and all muscle).

ALL MUSCLE!

"How did we get so much stuff?" April grumbled, plonking the pile on the grass outside the cabin and brushing off her purple jacket, which was currently more dust gray than plum purple.

April didn't mind cleaning so much as she thought there were a million other things—getting badges, climbing

mountains, solving mysteries—that they, Roanoke cabin, could be doing INSTEAD of cleaning.

What is cleaning if not looking at a bunch of stuff you already know about? she thought.

A puff of dust, like a giant cough, plumed out of Roanoke cabin's door, followed by Molly, who was rolling a boulder of stuff down the stairs. Molly's boulder looked like a meteor that had traveled extensively through space and collected, on its path, a mix of cosmic debris, all while hurtling toward the earth.

Actually, it was stuff that Molly and Bubbles, Molly's raccoon and hat, had just pulled out from under Molly's bunk. With great combined effort.

At home, Molly had to do a cleanup every day, so once in a blue moon didn't seem too bad. Also, Molly was not one to grumble, generally.

Molly was more of a blusher than a grumbler. And when Molly blushed, her whole face went the color of a tomato. Which was really embarrassing.

Molly's mystery meteor bounced down the stairs and onto the grass, where it collapsed in a heap next to April's pile with a soft *PFFFT* sound. Almost like it had given up on the idea of being a meteor, right at that moment.

"What the literal junk!" April exclaimed, looking at Molly.

"The weird thing is, I don't even recognize this junk," Molly said, holding her hands up near her face in a "Geez, I don't know" gesture. Molly's green baseball tee was also covered in dust. "I think maybe some of this is Bubbles's."

Bubbles the raccoon, who was so covered in dust he looked like a gray cat, blinked innocently, reached surreptitiously (which means in a way that is trying to avoid notice) into the wad, pulled out a pawful of nuts, and scampered back into the cabin to deposit them under Molly's bed.

Minutes later, Jo emerged from the cabin with her cleanup items: a small pile of folded notes that she had discovered tucked into one of the books next to her bed and two tiny silver screws she had found under her pillow.

"Wait." April shook her head in disbelief. "Is THAT all your junk?"

Jo didn't like to think of anything as junk, since Jo knew just about everything had a possible use.

"This is my recycling," she noted, neatly sliding her pile of papers into the recycling bin and pocketing the screws in one of her many pockets.

Beyond reusing whatever could be reused, Jo also liked to keep things tidy. At home, in her science lab, everything was neatly labeled and ordered. Because science is also generally neat and ordered. Even if the things you're researching . . . aren't.

Ripley liked to think of herself as sort of a tidy person.

Ripley liked to keep her clothes on the floor, but this did not mean Ripley was not a tidy person. A person can be a person who leaves their shirt on the floor so it is easier to slip into said shirt in the morning and still be a tidy person. Ripley's sister, who shared a room with her at home, disagreed.

Mostly what Ripley found when she went spelunking under her bunk was lots of glitter, which seemed to have rained down from her mattress and formed a thin layer of sparkle on the floor.

Which then got all over Ripley.

So Ripley's cleanup was walking outside covered in glitter and bouncing up and down until all the glitter came off, forming a sort of shimmery halo around her. Like a rainbow, only better.

"Aw," Molly said, looking over. "You're so sparkly! Where's your garbage?"

"Don't have any!" Ripley chirped.

"Keep cleaning!" Jen called over as she marched between cabins. "All library books should go back to the library! All odds and ends should go to the craft pile. All garbage goes in a landfill, so think very carefully before you put it in the garbage. Recycle! Reuse! CLEAN!"

"How come I have so much stuff?" April asked no one

in particular, putting one foot on her pile. "This is a truly Sisyphean task, my friends."

The classic Sisyphean task involved rolling a rock up a hill, watching the rock roll down the hill, and then rolling it back up again. Not exactly like cleaning a cabin, but both can feel kind of endless.

The pile under April's foot burbled and slowly began sucking in her shoe.

"AUGH!" April jumped back. "The pile! The pile has a mind of its own!!"

"Hey," Ripley said, dusting glitter off her hands, "so I was visiting my eggs today."

"Your aunts?" Jo asked, looking closely at one of the screws from her pocket and trying to decide where, exactly, it had come from.

"Eggs," Ripley repeated.

"Hey, look, you guys!" Mal stepped out of the cabin with what looked like, and was, a massive tumbleweed. "I looked under my bunk and I found . . . socks!"

"It's a Lumberjane miracle," Jo said.

"Are they YOUR socks?" Molly asked.

"Geez." Mal dropped the pile on the grass. "It's been so long since I've seen them, I don't even know."

Mal bent over and shook the dust out of her short black hair and off the many buttons on her vest.

At home, Mal's room was sometimes so messy she could roll out of bed and onto the floor and not even know it.

"A nest full of eggs," Ripley said, turning to April, who was now elbow deep in her pile.

"Hey!" April yanked her hand out of her pile and held up a tattered paperback. "Check it! It's my copy of *Tales from the Mermaid City*!"

It was an issue of the Mermaid Lemonade Stand series April had already read, many times, but it was a good one.

"Did you say Annette?" Molly looked up from rummaging through her pile, which WAS, it turns out, mostly acorns that Bubbles had been stowing under her bed. A cloud of dust hovered around Molly's head like a little private storm cloud. "Who's Annette?"

"A nest," Ripley said, again. Repeating herself. Again.

Molly stuck her finger in her ear and shook her head. "My ears are full of dust, you guys."

Ripley frowned.

Sometimes when you are smaller, the things you say are just not as big as the rest of the stuff going on.

Or at least this is how it seems when you are Ripley-size or a Ripley-like person.

Ripley was used to this as someone who got ready for school every morning in a house full of brothers and sisters who were older and louder than she was.

"What, sweetie?" was sort of Ripley's second name at home.

It was okay, but it was still kind of annoying.

Molly smiled, bending down to look at Ripley's frowning glittery face. "A nest sounds cooler than Annette," she said.

Ripley nodded. And opened her mouth to say more, but then, as often happens at a place where lots of stuff is happening all the time, there was a sudden clanging.

"CAMPERS! TIDY UP AND MEET AT THE MESS HALL FOR A BIG ANNOUNCEMENT!" Jen bellowed into her shiny megaphone.

"Tell me about it later," Molly whispered.

Ripley nodded, her face still glittery, especially on the bridge of her nose.

"Oooooooh. A big announcement." April whistled, abandoning her mysterious pile for a new adventure. "SOUNDS BIG!"

"Big relative to what?" Jo asked, striding with her big strides to the mess hall.

"BIG!" Ripley danced past them in a fog of leftover iridescence. "Let's go!"

EARN YOUR BY-THE-BOOK BADGE BY READING
ALL THE LUMBERJANES NOVELS!

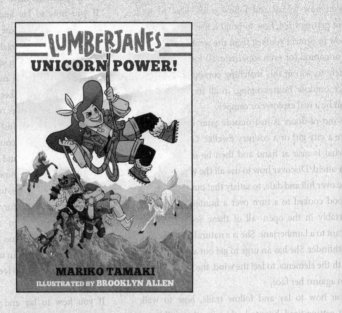

LIKED THIS BOOK?
THEN CHECK OUT *THE BACKSTAGERS*!

MARIKO TAMAKI

is a writer known for her graphic novel
This One Summer, a Caldecott Honor and
Printz Honor winner, cocreated with
her cousin Jillian Tamaki, among
other notable novels. See her work at
marikotamaki.blogspot.com.

BROOKLYN ALLEN

is a cocreator and the original illustrator
of the Lumberjanes graphic novel series,
and a graduate of the Savannah College
of Art and Design. Brooklyn's website is
brooklynaallen.tumblr.com.